Your Life, but sweeter!

Enjoy all the books in the
Your Life, but . . . series!

Your Life, but Better!

Your Life, but Cooler!

Your Life, but Sweeter!

Your Life, but Sweeter!

A novel by

CRYSTAL VELASQUEZ

Delacorte Press

This is a work of fiction. All incidents and dialogue, and all characters with the exception of some well-known historical and public figures, are products of the author's imagination and are not to be construed as real. Where real-life historical or public figures appear, the situations, incidents, and dialogues concerning those persons are fictional and are not intended to depict actual events or to change the fictional nature of the work. In all other respects, any resemblance to persons living or dead is entirely coincidental.

Text copyright © 2010 by Crystal Velasquez
Cover art copyright © 2010 by Angela Martini

All rights reserved. Published in the United States by Delacorte Press, an imprint of Random House Children's Books, a division of Random House, Inc., New York.

Delacorte Press is a registered trademark and the colophon is a trademark of Random House, Inc.

Visit us on the Web! www.randomhouse.com/kids

Educators and librarians, for a variety of teaching tools, visit us at www.randomhouse.com/teachers

Library of Congress Cataloging-in-Publication Data is available upon request.

ISBN 978-0-385-74038-8 (trade) — ISBN 978-0-375-89913-3 (ebook)

Printed in the United States of America

10 9 8 7 6 5 4 3 2 1

First Edition

Random House Children's Books supports the First Amendment and celebrates the right to read.

To my grandparents,
David and Guillermina White,
for your deep love, kindness,
strength, and generous sharing
of chocolate-chip cookies

And to my niece and nephew,
Eli and Jasmine Velasquez,
the apples of my eye

Acknowledgments

Even though my name is on the cover of this book, to say I wrote it alone would be a big fat lie. Stephanie Elliott, you are truly an excellent editor. I'm not sure that I would ever have written these books without your help and encouragement. Thank you for being so unbelievably awesome. Your new baby is one lucky little girl.

Again, I must thank Krista Vitola, the editorial assistant with the mostest. I'm so glad you've been involved with this series. Thank you to copy editor Ashley Mason for doing another great job and fixing all my embarrassing mistakes. Thank you to Tamar Schwartz, managing editor; Marci Senders, designer; Natalia Dextre, production associate; Colleen Fellingham, associate copy chief; Barbara Perris, copy chief; Meg O'Brien, publicist; Alyssa Sheinmel, marketing manager; and the entire Delacorte Press team. You have all gone above and beyond to make these books successful and I am forever in your debt.

Thank you to Angela Martini for her adorable cover illustrations, Dan Elliott for a wonderful author photo, and Maria Flores for creating my website. (Thanks also to Maria and her husband, Jason, for letting me spend a few days at their beautiful house in the mountains, where I wrote the first two chapters of this book. The peace and quiet helped!)

Thank you to Debi Lampert Rudman, the event coordinator at the Barnes & Noble in Princeton, NJ, where I had my first ever author appearance, for making me feel like a rock star. Thanks to Shona, Maria, Helen, Julie, and Phil for attending! Huge thanks to Bina Valenzano and Christine Freglette for inviting me to their lovely store in Brooklyn, The BookMark Shoppe. And to all the kids who participated in their choose-your-adventure writing contest, I'm so proud of you! It was a ton of fun to meet you all, and I hope you keep writing! And thanks to Dionne, Derek, Maria, Shona, and Jen for being there.

Ellen Scordato, thank you for interviewing me for your top-notch grammar blog on BN.com. I feel so famous! Thank you to the fine folks at the Watchung Booksellers in Montclair, NJ, for inviting me to be a part of your Writing Matters series, and to the Princeton Public Library for letting me participate in your annual Children's Book Festival. I am honored. I would also like to thank Aisha, my first official fan in California, for actually reading my blog!

Thanks to Madelin Velasquez, who spent several hours helping me figure out the outline. You're the best, Mom. And I'm so proud of you for going back to college! Camille Dewing-Vallejo gave me lots of great ideas for places to send the characters in New York City and gave me some fun quiz ideas too—even when she was home sick and had no voice. She also called me when I was at my most stressed to give me a much-needed pep talk. Thank you! Tom Wengelewski insisted that I use a particular feature of Times Square, which I did. Great advice. Dereeka Minks

Marte spent an afternoon at Dave and Buster's brainstorming with me (and a few phone calls after that). If not for the four of you, I might have pulled out all my hair. And thank you to my father, Eliezer Velasquez, who passed down his creativity and is the kindest, most amazing man I know. Love you, Dad. Love you too, big brother Eli! Thank you for being so supportive of my writing, and for making the best tents ever when we were kids. You helped show me how to use my imagination. Thanks to all my friends, who buy multiple copies of my books and make me laugh every day. I'm so lucky to know you all.

Thank you to the ladies of the Aegean Arts Circle Writing Workshop in Greece. I learned so much from all of you! And to the readers: I can't thank you enough for choosing my books. I'm happy to occupy even a small space on your shelf.

chapter ONE

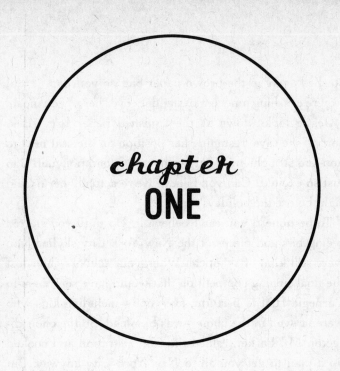

"There it is!" Jessie Miller shouts. "The Empire State Building! And it's all lit up in red and green!"

She leans over you to get her face as close to the bus's window as possible, flattening the last bit of bagel you had stashed away in the brown paper bag on your lap. "Hey! You're crushing innocent bystanders over here," you moan.

Jessie looks down at the squished paper bag. "Eek, sorry," she says, resuming her position on the seat next to you and straightening out her bouncy blond ponytail. "I'm just so excited! Can you believe we're actually here? And right before the holidays too!"

To be honest, you can't believe it. Up until you started seeing bits and pieces of the New York City skyline, you were still kind of skeptical. When your school's choir lost the final singing competition that would have sent them to Carnegie Hall to perform, everyone—including kids who weren't even in the choir—was bummed. So the choir director, Mr. Parker, rallied the administration and cooked up a plan to get you all to New York City anyway. But even though everybody in your grade has been doing fund-raisers for weeks to go on this trip (if you never hear the words "bake sale" or "car wash" again, it'll be too soon), you secretly thought your teachers would pull the old bait and switch and you'd end up at an exhibit *about* New York City at a local museum instead of seeing the real thing. But there was no shadiness involved at all. You're even meeting a couple of classes from a sister school in New York. (Mona won't shut up about that part. Apparently, a boy named Paul Renner, who used to live next door to her when she and her mom lived in the city, is one of the kids coming on the trip. According to Mona, he worships the ground she walks on. Just what you need—another Mona groupie.)

After what seems like forever inside a dark winding tunnel, the bus emerges back into the daylight, and you are officially in New York City. And not a moment too soon! The first hour on the bus was kind of fun, but after a while those seats start to feel a lot like concrete, and your butt could use a break. Although that will mean braving the cold outside the warm, heated bus. Brrr!

"Yeah, this is going to be awesome," you agree, as the bus rattles its way uptown through the early-morning traffic. "For one of us, anyway." You tap the top of Lena Saldano's head as you add the last part.

Lena, your other best friend, turns around and peeks over the back of the seat in front of you so that all you can see is her big brown eyes and matching hair. "Now, now, I can't help it if I have high-powered connections in New York."

"High-powered connections?" Amy Choi squeaks from across the aisle. She leans toward the three of you, her dark brown eyes brimming with curiosity. "Who? Somebody famous? Tell me, tell me!"

"Relax, Amy," you say, resisting the urge to call her Perez. (If anyone could take the gossip crown away from Perez Hilton, it would be Amy.) "Lena's just talking about her cousin Amanda. She goes to school here in the city."

"Not just any school," Lena insists, her eyes growing larger. "An Ivy League school! She's pre-law at Columbia."

"Oh," Amy says, turning around immediately. Nothing juicy about a cousin doing well in college and heading for law school. But you can tell that Lena is superproud. If she could skip ahead to college right now, she would. Amanda is a total rock star in her book.

"Anyway, I haven't seen her since she moved to New York and she felt bad about not being around for my last birthday. So she wants to spend the day with me."

"But doesn't she have classes?" you ask.

"No, she's taking her last final of the semester this morning. She did say something about having to go to her job later, though. I bet she interns at a big-time law firm and I won't even recognize her because she'll be wearing a three-piece suit and carrying a briefcase! We probably won't even get to do that much, since she'll be called away to consult on some big important case."

"Still, getting to see more of the city, even for a little while, sounds awesome." Jessie sighs wistfully. "I still can't believe Amanda got Ms. Darbeau to agree to let you leave the school trip. She must be a magician *and* a law student. Where is she going to take you, anyway?"

Lena shrugs. "Beats me. She said something about 'hopping a train and seeing where the day takes us.' Maybe I'll get to see her campus. And maybe a bunch of other campuses! There are so many schools here. NYU, FIT, Baruch . . ." Lena turns around slowly in her seat, visions of Barnard and Columbia dancing in her head.

"That's great for her," Jessie whispers to you, "but we're stuck. I was hoping to get in some quality celeb watching while we're here. I mean, hellooo, MTV films right in

Times Square. And I read on his Facebook fan page that Nick Jonas will be there today! Plus there are loads of famous people who live in Greenwich Village. There's so much we could do if we could sneak away on our own! But just look at this itinerary we actually have to follow." Jessie unfolds a crumpled piece of paper from the back pocket of her jeans. "There's hardly anything on it. And according to this, we'll be spending half our time in a ginormous museum!"

It's true. Since the art teacher, Ms. Darbeau, had a hand in planning the trip, the Metropolitan Museum of Art is the first thing on the menu—not that you could possibly have enough time to see it all. After that you'll be having lunch in the museum's cafeteria, followed by an hour and a half at the Sony Wonder Technology Lab, less than an hour at the Rockefeller Center ice-skating rink, and a show at Radio City Music Hall. "Actually," you tease Jess, "we won't even get to do the few things on this list. The Metropolitan Museum of Art alone will probably take all day!"

"Oh, great," Jessie says miserably. "That makes me feel *way* better."

You giggle and nudge her with your shoulder.

"Just kidding. Besides, the museum might be kind of cool."

"Yeah, maybe. But here's what *I* had in mind!" She pulls out her purse and extracts a tiny little pink square. She unfolds it to reveal a piece of lined paper filled to the brim with Jessie's curly purple handwriting. You take it from her and begin to read.

"'See every Broadway show; Madame Tussauds wax museum; shop at Henri Bendel, Bloomingdale's, Saks Fifth Avenue, and Tiffany's; have lunch in Little Italy; tour MTV Studios and *meet Nick Jonas*!!!' "—this last one is underlined three times—"'go to the top of the Empire State Building; visit Dylan's Candy Bar; poetry slam in Greenwich Village; horse-and-carriage ride in Central Park . . .' " The list continues, but you run out of breath. "Jess," you say with a laugh, shaking the paper in her face. "You would need to be here for a month to do all this stuff!"

"And win the lottery," Lena's voice shoots over the bus seat. "Twice."

Jessie shrugs. "A girl can dream," she replies, refolding the piece of paper and putting it in her purse. "But the Nick Jonas thing is totally possible. Or at least *some* celebrity. All we have to do is keep our eyes peeled! Promise you will."

You shake your head and sigh. "I'm not sure I should support your obvious celeb addiction, but fine, I promise." Jessie smiles, satisfied. But really, you just hope New York is as glam as you picture it in your mind. You and your mom have started having classic movie nights together, and not too long ago you watched *Breakfast at Tiffany's*, starring Audrey Hepburn. Now, there was a woman with style! Since then, you've totally had a fantasy of gallivanting around the town in a chic black dress and pumps, a string of pearls, a slick tan trench coat, and black sunglasses that cover half your face. It seems like the right outfit to wear while shopping at pricey boutiques and fancy salons. Too bad in reality you're wearing a superthick blue parka, warm boots, and the blue and green knit cap your grandmother made for you last winter, complete with an embarrassing pom-pom on top. And you only have enough money to buy a few souvenirs, and we're talking plastic snow globes, not diamond earrings. Oh well. Like Jessie said, a girl can dream.

At last the bus pulls up behind a caravan of other buses and parks in front of the Metropolitan Museum of Art. (You overhear Mona telling Lisa Topple that no one calls it that. *Real* New Yorkers—and she's including herself in that group—just call it "the Met." Ugh. You hope she's not going to be bragging like this all day.) As you climb out of the bus and start lining up on the stairs leading to the entrance, your gym teacher, Mr. Nocera, who you assume they invited along because he was once a drill sergeant in the army, checks you all off on his clipboard and blows his whistle to make sure you're in a straight line. Even though Mr. Nocera is kind of a cutie, you can already tell you're going to hate that whistle by the end of the day. *Jeez, is this going to be a fun trip or boot camp?* you think. The other kids grumble, probably thinking the same thing. But after you pass through the threshold into the gigantic lobby, everyone is speechless—especially Jimmy Morehouse, who you catch a glimpse of near the back of the line next to Charlie Daniels. While Ms. Darbeau goes off to speak to a museum rep and the other teachers, Jimmy cranes his neck to look up at the ceiling, which seems like it's about a million miles away, it's so high. After Jimmy's successful art debut not too long ago at the local community center, he has seemed a lot more confident about his dream of becoming an artist. He sketches all the time now, and his determination makes you like him even more.

For some reason you'd thought your school would have the run of the place today, but there are people everywhere—some browsing through the pamphlets at the big round information booth in the middle of the lobby, some thumbing through books in the gift shop, and some gathering around the small group of musicians playing classical music in the far corner. Even Jessie has to admit it's pretty awesome.

"All right, kids," Ms. Darbeau says, clapping her hands quickly to get your attention. "As you know, we are on a tight schedule today, so we can't possibly see as much of this museum as I—uh, you—would like. So we will be taking a self-guided tour through the Egyptian artifacts and then moving on to view the Picasso collection."

At that, Jimmy's ears perk up beneath his wavy brown hair, and his deep green eyes have a sudden twinkle in them. Picasso is his favorite, and he reacts to this news the way other kids might respond if someone told them that they'd be spending the day at the beach. His inner artist is geeking out big-time, and it's adorable.

After you all turn in your heavy winter coats at the coat

check and Lena texts her cousin to let her know where she'll be, Ms. Darbeau leads your group through the dimly lit rooms full of Egyptian art. The glazed bowls look just as good as anything you'd find in IKEA. But the giant statues of ancient pharaohs who look a little like lions take your breath away.

Jessie nudges you and Lena. "Hey, don't you think that one kind of looks like—"

"Nick Jonas?" Lena finishes for Jessie.

"Yeah, how'd you know?"

"Because thou art afflicted with Jonas fever," Lena says gently, touching Jessie's shoulder as if breaking the news that she has some fatal disease. "You've already seen his visage in a painted vase, a coffin lid, and a cave painting. The situation is dire! Recover and spare us this folly!"

Jessie looks to you to decipher Lena's Elizabethan English once again.

"In other words, snap out of it!"

Jessie has to laugh at herself, which starts you and Lena giggling too. "Okay, you're right. I just can't help it! Knowing that he and I are in the same city right now is driving me insane."

"We know. And you're taking us with you!" Lena finishes. You all laugh and are heading toward the giant tombs when a girl comes running up to you three, her dark brown hair swept up into a messy bun and her jeans worn and faded. She looks like an older, slightly more disheveled version of Lena.

"There you are!" she says, and sweeps Lena up into a twirling hug. Ah. She must be Amanda. So much for the three-piece suit and briefcase, though. If she is interning at a law firm, she's taking casual Fridays to the extreme. "I've been looking for you for a while, but I think I got turned around somewhere near the Temple of Dendur and ended up back in the lobby. I forgot how big this place is!"

"That's okay," Lena says quickly, giving her cousin a final squeeze. "It's so awesome to see you!" After Lena introduces you and Jessie, she grabs Amanda's hand and leads her to Ms. Darbeau to let her know she's leaving.

"Oh well, there she goes, off to see real live people while we're stuck in here with the mummies," Jessie says glumly.

"Aw, come on, it's not so bad," you offer. "At least we . . ." You were going to make a joke about not having to battle an army of skeletons or anything like in the *Mummy* movies. But you're distracted when you see Amanda handing Ms. Darbeau two sheets of paper and pointing at you and Jessie. Ms. Darbeau reads them, nods, and calls you two over with a quick wave of her index and middle fingers. Uh-oh. Are you guys in trouble or something? Has your giggling disturbed the ancient mummies and now you're being kicked out?

With Jessie inching along just behind you, you walk haltingly over to Lena, Amanda, and your art teacher, fearing the worst. "Y-yes?"

Ms. Darbeau hands you the two letters—one from your parents and one from Jessie's. "It seems that Amanda here has obtained written permission from both your parents to leave the school trip and go with Amanda and Lena if you like. I did speak to your parents earlier but they wanted it to be a surprise, and I would not allow you to go without permission in writing. Now that I have that, the choice is yours." Amanda is beaming. If you didn't know better, you'd think Lena looks a little less excited, but maybe you're imagining that.

"Seriously?" Jessie squeals and jumps up and down. "Sweet!" Realizing that she might seem a little too gleeful in front of Ms. Darbeau, who you all know worked really hard to plan this trip, Jessie quickly calms down and tries to wipe the broad smile off her delicate face. "Oh, uh, I just mean I'd rather see this whole place or none of it at all, so maybe I'll just come back another time when I can spend loads and loads of hours."

"Mm-hm," Ms. Darbeau says shortly, not buying a word of that. "And what about you?" she says, turning toward you. This might have been a no-brainer for Jessie, but as usual, for you it's a little more complicated.

At long last you're in New York City! Even better, you get to be here with your closest friends in the world, Lena and Jessie, and your long-time crush, Jimmy Morehouse. Sure, you've had fantasies about ditching the trip and exploring the city on your own, but you never thought you'd

actually get to. But now that the opportunity has presented itself, you're just not sure. At least with your school, you know what you're in for. But who knows how your day will go if you leave with Amanda? Are you a free spirit who can handle the unexpected, or would you rather stick with the routine and avoid the pitfalls that might come? Take the quiz and find out!

QUIZ TIME!

Circle your answers and tally up the points at the end.

1. **You and your friends want to go see the latest blockbuster movie that's coming out in a few weeks. You're in charge of securing the tix. What do you do?**
   - **A.** Scope out which theaters will be playing the flick, research which one has the best snacks and sound system, order the tickets weeks in advance, and arrange to be at the theater at least two hours before showtime to make sure you and your buds are the first ones in and can have your choice of seats. Your friends think it's overkill, but they'll thank you later!
   - **B.** Buy the tickets over the Internet the day before the movie opens and have your friends meet up an hour before the start time to snag a good place on line.
   - **C.** Show up at the theater a little early to buy your tickets and hope your friends can all find decent seats. (You might have to sit in the dreaded first row!)
   - **D.** Go to the first theater you see and show up right at start time to buy tickets. You hate to wait around and it's more

exciting to do things at the last minute. Sure, the show might be sold out, but if it is, you'll just see something else.

2. **If you had your choice of any kind of vacation, you would choose:**

   A. a preplanned guided tour in Europe. That way you wouldn't have to worry about figuring out where to go each day, how to get there, or when to go. Everything would be planned out in advance, so all you'd have to do is sit back and enjoy.

   B. a trip you and your family have taken many times before. You always stay at the same place and do the same things, and it's always awesome.

   C. any one of the itineraries in a travel book. Someone else has already tried them out so you'll know exactly what to do.

   D. going to the airport and getting on the first plane out. Then you'd stay at whatever hotels you come across. It would be so fun to fly by the seat of your pants and just see where you end up!

3. **Your parents have finally broken down and gotten you the puppy you've always wanted. But he's a little wild, running around everywhere and chewing up everything he sees. What's your doggy-training style?**

   A. You ask to get the puppy enrolled in obedience school as soon as possible. By the time he comes back, he should be trained almost well enough to be a police dog. A new puppy is most fun when he's perfectly behaved.

B. You train him to do the basics so that he won't be a neighborhood menace. Thanks to you, the puppy will be able to sit, speak, and roll over on command—and won't even *think* about biting the mail carrier.

C. You train him to let you know when he needs to go out and if he's hungry. Everything else is gravy.

D. Training? That's so formal. Why try to stifle a new puppy's spirit? It's way more fun to see him jump and play with no boundaries at all (even if that means cleaning up the occasional puddle).

4. **When it comes to your Facebook profile, you prefer to:**

A. keep it private so that only a select group of friends and family can see it. *And* you customize all your lists so that only some of those people can see your pictures and interests. *And* you only post things that you don't mind the whole world seeing—which isn't a lot. *And* . . .

B. add all your friends from school and your family members. But don't add friends of friends who you don't know. You don't want your friends list getting too out of control and you definitely don't want any apps like Farmville that you'd have to depend on other people to maintain.

C. keep your profile private, but add almost everyone who asks. The more the merrier!

D. keep your profile public and add anyone who wants to be friends, even if they're strangers. Why limit yourself? The world would be better if everyone were friends.

5. **Because you've gotten the best grades in the school, your principal asks you to speak for about three minutes at this year's graduation ceremony. What an honor! How do you prepare?**

A. You read up on other graduation speeches, collect some meaningful quotes you can use, plan out everything you're going to say, and time your speech so that it's exactly three minutes long. You even write in your notes when you should make certain hand gestures or when to pause. You don't want to leave anything to chance!

B. You write your speech in advance and practice a few times in the mirror, but then don't stress too much about it. You don't want to seem too rehearsed.

C. You jot down some general notes the night before so that you remember to say a few important things. But then you'll just speak from your heart.

D. Why prepare something? It'll be a lot more heartfelt if you just go up there and wing it, saying whatever it is you feel at the moment.

Give yourself 1 point for every time you answered **A**, 2 points for every **B**, 3 points for every **C**, and 4 points for every **D**.

—If you scored between 5 and 12, go to page 25.

—If you scored between 13 and 20, go to page 36.

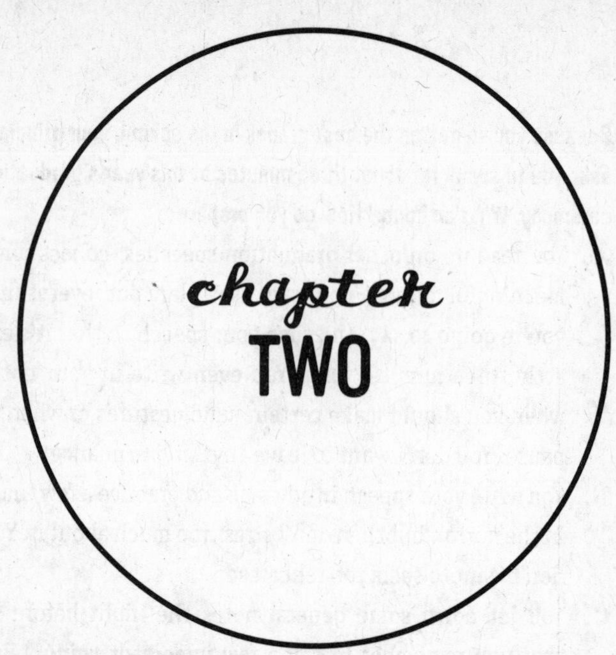

chapter TWO

You're a free spirit! You go with the program when you must, but you'd much rather be set loose to discover the world on your own and you're always up for an adventure. You don't like to tie anyone else down with rules because you don't want to be tied down either. It's wonderful to be so open and flexible. Just remember that sometimes a little preparation can help you avoid trouble along the way.

You hem and haw . . . for about twenty seconds. Of course you want to go with your friends! Ms. Darbeau's itinerary sounds good, but getting to see the rest of the city without having to stay in a single-file line like a soldier in Mr. Nocera's army? Well, you just can't pass that up.

Before you go, though, you tap your favorite artist on the shoulder.

"Huh?" Jimmy turns around. He'd been staring at a row of hieroglyphics behind a thick glass case. When he sees you, he smiles sweetly and rubs the back of his head. "Oh, hey. This is pretty cool, huh?" he says. "Can you believe they had to make their own paint back then by grinding colorful objects? Crazy . . ."

"Yeah, it is." You smile back, loving the fact that Jimmy is so into learning. For a moment, you're tempted to stay again. But when you glance back at Jessie, she is bouncing up and down on her tippy toes and pointing at an imaginary watch on her wrist. *Hurry up,* she mouths.

Okay, you mouth back.

"So . . . I'm taking off now, Jimmy."

His sweet smile wilts a little and he furrows his dark eyebrows in confusion. "Taking off? Where?"

You point back at Amanda. "Lena's cousin got permission to take us out for the day. I don't know where to, but it should be fun."

"Oh." He looks down at his Nikes so you can't see his face. "Okay, well, have fun, I guess."

"Thanks," you say. "I'll talk to you later, though, right?"

"Yeah, later," Jimmy mumbles and turns back to the hieroglyphics. "I hope you have a blast." The words are right, but you can tell by the way he says them that he's a little disappointed, maybe even a little mad?

Oh well. Even though you can't stand the thought of Jimmy being upset, you can't worry about that right now. New York City awaits!

After retrieving your coats, you, Lena, Jessie, and Amanda leave the massive museum and cross Fifth Avenue heading for the train station a few blocks away. You and your friends are loving this.

Poor Amanda can hardly walk two feet before one of you begs her to stop and take your picture in front of something. First you wanted to pose with one of the doormen from a swanky apartment building. He was wearing a black uniform with gold tassels and shiny leather shoes, and he seemed only too happy to say "cheese." Then you took a picture of Lena eating a real New York City hot dog from a street vendor. And just before you ducked into the Lexington Avenue train station, you saw a man dressed as Santa Claus ringing a heavy brass bell. Lena smiled as you snapped a picture of her throwing change into his bucket for the Salvation Army. You know you've walked only a few blocks, but your first impression of New York City = love at first sight!

The three of you are still buzzing as you walk down the steps into the dark train station on Eighty-sixth Street. Amanda stops at a MetroCard machine to buy you all subway passes for the day—apparently, all of your parents sent Amanda enough money to entertain you for a few hours, within reason, of course—and one by one you swipe the thin plastic cards through a slot and walk through the turnstiles that lead you onto the crowded subway platform.

"Cool! Our first ride on a subway," Jessie gushes. "I heard a lot of celebrities in New York ride the trains because it's more environmentally friendly than taking limos everywhere they go."

"That's actually true," Amanda agrees. "I saw Drew Barrymore on the N train once."

"Get out!" Jessie yells, startling the people standing near her. You all laugh.

Amanda smiles and says, "Listen, I'm going to go buy a paper from that candy stand at the end of the platform." She points. "That way we can read up on the events going on around the city today. Do me a favor and stay put." She turns to Jessie. "And don't scare away the other passengers."

"Who, me?" Jessie bats her eyelashes innocently. "Not a chance."

Amanda grins and walks away, shaking her head.

"Lena, your cousin is so cool," you say sincerely. "Not many college kids would want to spend a whole day with a bunch of thirteen-year-olds. Especially a loud-mouthed troublemaker like this one," you add, throwing your arm affectionately around Jessie's shoulder. "It's really awesome of her to do this. Why didn't you tell us, though? You must've been in on the surprise."

"Actually, I wasn't." Lena shrugs. "I kind of thought it would be just me and Amanda. But this is cool too." Lena smiles, but did you detect a hint of sadness just now? Before you have a chance to find out, you feel the platform start to rumble.

"Uh, guys? New York doesn't have earthquakes, does it?"

"I don't think so," Jessie answers. "But it sure feels like one."

"Relax," Lena says smoothly. "It's just the train. It's headed this way. See? Look at the light coming down the tunnel."

Honestly, you can't see much of anything, there are so many people standing all around you. And as the train gets closer and closer, the wall of people starts to close in, moving you toward the platform. Finally the train darts out of the tunnel and pulls into the station—at first with lightning speed, and then slowing to a crawl until you hear a puff of air as the doors slide open. What happens next goes by so quickly, it's almost like you're dreaming it.

After the doors open, there's a trickle of passengers getting off the train, and then the crowd of people on the platform surges forward, spilling into the car like a tidal wave—and the wave is taking you and your friends along! All three of you are swept into the train, squished between men in suits and teenagers in down-filled coats.

"Amanda!" you hear Lena cry out. "Help!"

You have been pushed toward the center of the car near a long narrow window, and you can see Amanda look up from the newspaper she just bought. She sees what's happening and comes running to the rescue, but just as she reaches your car, the bell dings again and the doors close abruptly, right in her face. She yells something, but none of you can hear it over the roar of the train as it goes sailing off into the tunnel to who knows where.

So how are you enjoying your trip to New York City so far? It's only been a couple of hours and already you've visited a museum that's bigger than thirty houses put together, you've seen some quintessential New York sights, and oh yeah, you got hijacked by a speeding train and separated from the one person who had any idea how to get around the Big Apple. Not to panic you or anything, but YIKES! You have total faith in yourself and your friends, but big cities can be dangerous and the truth is, you're all newbies here. Anything could happen! In this situation, you clearly need help. But can you admit that and actually ask for it? Or are you convinced you can figure this out on your own? If you need help answering these questions, you'd better take this quiz.

QUIZ TIME!

Circle your answers and tally up the points at the end.

1. **You have been struggling with your science class for months and your big final exam is coming up. What do you do?**

   A. Ask your parents to get you a professional tutor ASAP. It's obvious to you that you're going to need to bring in the big guns if you want to pass this class.

B. Ask a group of kids who are doing well in the class to help you after school. In exchange maybe you can help them in a class that's giving them trouble.

C. Try to study on your own and then have your best friend quiz you to see if you've gotten it down.

D. Study hard and just do the best you can on your own. You don't really want it to be public knowledge that you're having such a hard time with the class.

2. **You're in a store searching for the perfect Mother's Day present, but you can't seem to find a thing. Finally a salesclerk asks you if you need help. You say:**

A. "Yes, please!" The salespeople know this store inside out and can surely help you find the perfect gift for your mom. What's the use of struggling on your own?

B. "Maybe." You tell her the kind of thing you're looking for and take her advice into consideration, but the final call is yours.

C. "Not yet." You'd rather look at every single thing in the store before you give up. You want to be able to tell your mom that the gift was all your idea.

D. "No, thanks." The salesclerk can't possibly know your mom better than you do, so there's no sense in wasting her time or yours. If you can't find a gift in here, then you'll figure something else out. (You hope.)

3. **You are typing away on your computer when all of a sudden the screen goes blank and it looks like all your files are gone! So of course you:**

A. call the computer tech support guys immediately. They've gotta help you get all your stuff back!

B. have your dad take a look and try to fix it. He knows a little about computers. Hopefully he can handle it.

C. consult your computer's guidebook. There's a whole troubleshooting section and the answer has *got* to be there.

D. press every button and reboot a hundred times to see if it helps. You have absolutely no idea how to fix it, but you'd hate to have to confess to your folks that you broke your computer somehow.

4. **You are having a pretty serious problem at home and it's starting to affect your schoolwork. How do you handle it?**

A. Request a meeting with your school's guidance counselor and tell her the situation. Her whole job is to help kids like you with whatever they're dealing with. And you definitely need the help.

B. Tell a trusted friend what you're going through and ask for her advice. She always seems to know the right thing to do.

C. You check out some websites online that discuss the kind of problems you're having. Maybe if you read about what someone else did, it'll give you an idea of what you should do.

D. Keep it to yourself and try to cope on your own. It's way too serious to tell anybody else. Maybe the problem will just go away in time.

5. **You promised to make three dozen cupcakes for your school's bake sale, which didn't sound like a lot at the time, but now it seems next to impossible. It's the night before the sale and you're nowhere near done. What do you do?**

A. Call all your friends over and offer to feed them pizza if they'll help you bake. You can use as many hands as you can get! And they're used to you asking them to pitch in.

B. Ask your folks to help you out. They may not want to spend all night baking, but you know they'll do it for you.

C. You make as many cupcakes as you can and then ask your parents if they'll buy some store-bought goodies to make up the difference.

D. You make as many cupcakes as you can before your bedtime and then call it a night. You know you're coming up short, but there are only so many hours in the day. The school will just have to deal.

Give yourself 1 point for every time you answered A, 2 points for every B, 3 points for every C, and 4 points for every D.

—If you scored between 5 and 12, go to page 36.

—If you scored between 13 and 20, go to page 44.

chapter THREE

Impressive! **Not everyone can admit that they like a little structure. You just don't see what's wrong with scheduling things in advance to make sure they run smoothly. Your friends may think you lack spontaneity, but thanks to you, you always have tickets to sold-out movies and always have a plan B just in case. You may not be a free spirit, but you rarely find yourself in situations you aren't prepared for, and that gives you peace of mind.**

Going off with Amanda is tempting, but who knows what you would end up doing? In your experience, unplanned outings end up turning into a big ol' mess. (Remember when you and Jessie decided to have a picnic in the park at the last minute and it started pouring and everything got soaking wet? Yeah. Like that.) At least if you stick with your class, you know you'll definitely get to see a few cool things. For all you know, Lena will talk Amanda into spending the whole day touring colleges and going over her blog.

"Sorry, guys," you say apologetically, pulling Jessie and Lena aside. "That sounds great, but I kind of want to see the Picasso exhibit."

"Ooooh, I get it," Jessie says, shooting a glance over at Jimmy, who is studying a wall of hieroglyphics. "The 'Picasso exhibit.' Right." She winks at you conspiratorially.

"What? No, it's not like that," you insist. Although you admit you have been looking forward to hanging with Jimmy in New York, that wouldn't stop you from going with Amanda if you really wanted to.

But Jessie has already made up her mind about your reasons. "Okay, whatever you say. Have fun." She winks once more and gives you a quick hug. "And text me with updates!"

You sigh, giving up on setting her straight.

"Are you sure you don't want to come?" Lena asks a final time.

"I'm sure."

"All right. Then wish us well as we venture forth into the abyss!"

And with that, Amanda and your friends are gone. But at least you've still got Jimmy, Charlie, and Lizette. Well, really just Jimmy, since Lena asked Lizette to fill in for her and help Charlie with the blog for the day while she's gone.

Since Charlie teamed up with Lena, the blog, which started out as a personal record to demonstrate her writing skills to future college recruiters, has turned into a bona fide school phenomenon. It's even more popular than the school paper—and almost as widely read as Amy's gossip-filled tweets. And since Lena's blog covers what's going on inside and outside the school (and isn't only about the popular kids), everybody loves it. (Thank goodness she took out some of the more secret stuff—like your crush on a certain someone—before she made the blog public.)

So while Charlie and Lizette busily take notes and pictures as they work their way through the museum, you're content to follow Jimmy around, talking about art and school and whatever else you can think of. You two talk pretty much nonstop . . . until you get to the Picasso exhibit, that is.

"Wow," Jimmy says as he enters the first room, which shows all of Picasso's earliest work, some of it done when he wasn't much older than Jimmy.

"So anyway, that history test last week was tough, right? I mean, I think it may have actually killed a few of my brain cells, I was concentrating so hard."

"Uh-huh," Jimmy says, barely looking at you.

"I mean, I'm thinking of running for class president just so I can get tests with three or more essay questions banned."

"Mm-hm," Jimmy grunts. "Yes, great."

Okay, he is totally ignoring you. And you can see why. Jimmy has his trusty sketchpad out and his hand is moving across it as if it's attached to a robotic arm instead of a klutzy thirteen-year-old with paint under his nails. Being around this many of his favorite artist's paintings has really gotten his creative juices flowing and right now, he barely notices that you're in the room.

Oh well. Guess you'll just have to wander off and check out the paintings on your own. You're staring at one huge canvas from Picasso's cubist period when someone steps up next to you, crosses his arms, and says, "What is that supposed to be?"

You glance over and see a boy you don't recognize. His jet-black hair and pale blue eyes are even more striking than some of the masterpieces you're surrounded by. You would definitely remember him if you'd seen him before. He must be from one of the New York schools.

"Well, it's a table, a bottle of wine, and a glass."

"Where?" he says, squinting and tilting his head to the side.

You have spent so much time with Jimmy that you actually know something about these paintings. If Jimmy were paying you any mind, he'd be proud to hear you say, "See this cube here? This represents the bottle, and this here is the stem of the glass. . . ." You show him all the elements, pointing from about a foot away. (Mark Bukowski has already been yelled at by one of the guards pacing the room not to get too close to the artwork, and there should *definitely* be no touching!)

"Dude, why didn't he just paint a real glass, bottle, and table? My six-year-old little brother could draw them better than this."

"Because," you say, getting a little defensive over one of your favorite pieces of art, "Picasso believed in breaking down shapes as much as he could without the object becoming unrecognizable." Whoa. You didn't even know that knowledge was in your brain!

"Huh," the boy grunts. "You really know your stuff. Maybe I should stick with you."

"Yeah, maybe," you say smoothly.

"Maybe *not*!" a shrill voice says behind you. Groan. You don't even have to turn around to see who it is. Mona Winston.

"Paul, where have you been?" Mona continues. "Your teacher has been looking for you. Your class has already moved on to the next room."

Paul? Oh no. This must be the infamous Paul that Mona has been bragging about all morning. And here you are, daring to talk to him.

"Aw, shoot, really?" Paul says, glancing into the next room. "Okay, thanks, Mona."

Mona smiles broadly, her perfect white teeth gleaming under the soft track lighting in the room. "Any time."

Paul turns to you and extends his hand, which you shake with your own. "I'll see you around," he says.

You nod dumbly as he strides away, rejoining his class.

When you look back at Mona's face, her usually flawless

alabaster skin is red and blotchy, and she's crossing her arms tightly over her chest. "Look, you'd better leave him alone," Mona orders. "Can't you see he doesn't want to talk to *you*?"

"Uh, actually, he talked to me first," you correct her. "What's it to you, anyway?"

"Just back off," Mona says fiercely. "Find someone else to bore to tears." With that she huffs and goes stalking away.

"That was awesome!" Amy Choi says, suddenly by your side.

"'Awesome' is not the word I would use," you say miserably. "What is her problem, anyway? Isn't he the guy that she said worships her and that she was going to have a hard time shaking? She should have been happy to see him talking to someone else."

Amy shakes her head and pulls out her phone. "You can't believe everything she says. You should know that by now. All that talk she was doing about Paul worshiping her is really because *she* worships *him*."

"No way." Mona isn't the only one you usually can't believe. Amy is like a professional gossip and doesn't always check her sources before she reports the news. She once spread the word that Lizette's twin cousins, Celia and Delia, weren't actually sisters because she'd heard one accuse the other of being adopted.

"I can prove it," Amy says smugly, clicking a few buttons on her phone and shoving the high-resolution screen in your face. In front of you is a picture taken over someone's shoulder. A fine, pale hand is holding a gel-tipped pen

(Mona's fave) and doodling over and over again: *MW + PR*. "I passed by her seat on the bus and clicked that when she wasn't looking. PR stands for Paul Renner. And you, my friend, were just caught flirting with him."

"But I wasn't!" you protest. "I was just talking to him."

"I guarantee you Mona doesn't see it that way."

Great.

You've never thought of yourself as a controversial person, and yet you seem to be causing controversy left and right. First you shock your friends by choosing to stick with your class trip instead of heading out on a New York City adventure. And then you manage to cause yet another classic Mona meltdown just by talking to someone. It turns out that Mona has an actual crush on a guy, which is news to you. But does that mean she gets to treat you like pond scum? It's hard to see things her way, but can you do it? Take the quiz and find out.

QUIZ TIME!

Circle your answers and tally up the points at the end.

1. **When you write short stories in your creative writing class, you like to include:**

   A. as many characters as you can. Half the fun of writing fiction is getting to explore lots of different personalities and figuring out what would motivate different characters.

B. a close-knit group of friends that you can base on your real-life friends. You know what makes your best buds tick, so it's easy to write about characters just like them.

C. two characters, tops. It's hard enough to get inside one character's mind. Two is about all you can handle.

D. one character that is pretty much based on you. It only makes sense that you would write from your own point of view.

2. **You're watching a really sad movie about a boy who finds out his dog is sick. How do you react?**

A. You cry like a baby. Even though you've never had a dog, you can imagine what it must feel like for someone you care about to get sick.

B. You're upset for the boy but stay dry-eyed. You're just thankful you're not going through that in real life.

C. You're a little sad because you hate to see sick animals. But you get over it as soon as the movie is over.

D. You don't feel much of anything. It's just a movie, after all.

3. **You're on a crowded bus on your way home, and the bus driver is going so fast that it seems like he's taking the turns on two wheels. Thank goodness you were lucky enough to score a seat. But the pregnant woman standing in front of you wasn't. You decide to:**

A. get up and offer her your seat immediately, not taking no for an answer. Just by looking at her, you can tell how uncomfortable she is, and you're betting her back is probably aching too. You know she'd be grateful to be able to rest her feet.

B. wait a few minutes to see if anyone else offers her a seat first. If they don't, you have no problem doing it. (It sure was nice sitting down for a while, though!)

C. halfheartedly offer her your seat, mumbling so that she can barely hear you. If she *can* hear you, you kind of hope she says, "No, thanks." After all, you're tired too. What makes her more deserving of a seat than you are?

D. pretend you're asleep. You don't want to feel pressured to give up your seat. And the woman looks healthy and strong, anyway. You're sure she's fine.

4. **You were chosen to be one of the captains in gym class today for a game of volleyball. As captain, you get to choose your teammates, two at a time. When it gets down to the last six, there are two great players, two okay players, and two girls who usually spend more time hiding from the ball than hitting it. You choose:**

A. the two girls who are volleyball pariahs. Being picked last stinks, and you would hate to do that to girls who get picked last all the time. That might seem like a terrible move to your teammates, but you think of it as an investment. You know they're scared, but you can turn these two into grade A players (or at least get them to the point where they don't duck every time the ball comes to them).

B. one of the great players and one player who needs work.

Who better than the great player for the weak player to learn from?

C. the two okay players. You want to win, but you don't want anyone to think it's just because your team is stacked.

D. the two great players, of course! You're all about forming the dream team, and anyone who stands in your way better watch out!

5. **Your five-year-old cousin Camille is going to be in a four-hour dance recital and she really wants you to come and see everyone in her dance school strut their stuff. Do you attend?**

A. Of course! You know how proud she is of her school and how good she'll feel if she looks out into the crowd and sees your smiling face—and maybe a giant poster saying *Go, Camille!* You also know how scared she'll be if she has to face the crowd alone. You'll stay from beginning to end and cheer as if you're watching the *American Idol* finale.

B. Well, sure. It's hard to say no to that cute little face. You'll go and stay until you see Camille perform. You may not stay the full four hours, but at least she'll know you were there.

C. If you must. You'll go and watch her part, but you pretty much fall asleep for the rest of it. (*Four hours?* Come on! Not even jazz hands would keep you awake for that many tap numbers.)

D. Doubt it. Sitting there for four hours is just cruel and unusual punishment. Besides, you've seen her practice a million times. No need for you to see it again onstage. You offer to pick her up afterward and do something you both consider fun, like buying some hot new shoes. Now, *that* you could spend four hours doing.

Give yourself 1 point for every time you answered **A**, 2 points for every **B**, 3 points for every **C**, and 4 points for every **D**.

—If you scored between 5 and 12, go to page 53.

—If you scored between 13 and 20, go to page 63.

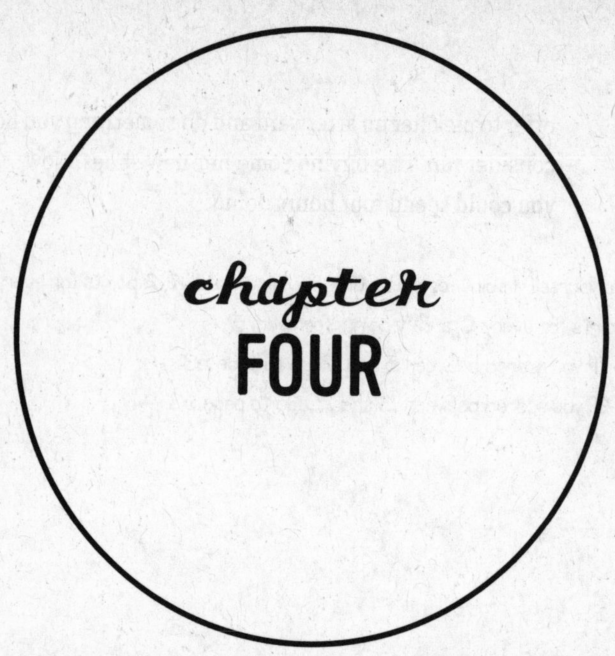

chapter FOUR

Good for you! **You're not too proud or afraid to ask for help when you really need it. You know that getting a hand now and then doesn't mean you're not capable, but that no one can do it all on their own. Just make sure you don't automatically seek help before you've even given it a try yourself. How will you ever know your limits if you don't test them out once in a while?**

"What do we do now?" Lena says in a panicky voice that is not at all like her. "We lost Amanda!"

"And we have no idea where to go, either," Jessie adds, biting her pale pink lips nervously.

Even worse, all the native New Yorkers around you seem

to know exactly what they're doing. Why are you three the only ones freaking out?

"Lena, can you call Amanda?"

"I tried," she says, sounding like she's about to cry. "But I'm not getting any cell phone reception down here."

"We need help," you say decisively. "We've got to get to that conductor." As you got shoved onto the train, you could see the conductor hanging casually in the window at the tiny room at the end of the car. You grab one of Lena's hands and tell her to grab Jessie's, nudging your way between the clusters of people packed like sardines between you and the conductor's booth. "Come on!" you say, totally taking charge.

It's a struggle, and you're pretty sure you step on a couple of feet along the way, but eventually you make it to the end of the car and knock on the shiny metal door.

After a minute, it swings open and a dark-skinned woman in a light blue shirt and black pants pokes her head out. "Yes?" She eyes you and your friends curiously.

"We need help," you blurt out. "Back at the last stop, we got separated from her cousin"—you point your thumb at Lena—"and now we can't even call her because we have no cell phone reception. What do we do?"

The conductor nods knowingly, as if this happens all the time. "Don't panic, girls. Just get out at the next stop and go upstairs so that you can call your cousin. Or I can call transit security instead."

"You mean the police?" Jessie screeches, her eyes going wide.

“That’s what I mean,” the conductor says, stifling a yawn and reaching for a walkie-talkie.

“No, that’s all right,” you tell her quickly. “We’ll try to call Amanda first. And if we can’t reach her, we’ll call the police.”

“All right, ladies,” the conductor answers, not looking too concerned. “Good luck.” With that she closes the metal door again, and minutes later the train pulls into the next station, Fifty-ninth Street and Lexington Avenue. Thankfully, lots of people get off here so you don’t have to fight too hard. You follow the Exit signs that lead up the stairs and out into the sunlight, where you finally allow yourself a deep breath.

Lena doesn’t waste any time before pulling out her phone and calling Amanda.

“What did she say to do?” you ask after Lena hangs up.

“She said to stay put—and she means it this time.”

“Got it,” you answer, looking around at the skyscrapers reaching into the sky all around you. Each one is decked out with colorful wreaths, and there is a light dusting of snow on the ground.

“Hey, hey!” Jessie suddenly shouts next to you. “Isn’t that Nick Jonas? No, can’t be. Wait, could be . . .”

She points to a boy with unruly black hair hurrying down the street in a pair of sunglasses and a stylish black wool coat. “I can’t really see his face, but it does kinda look like him, I guess . . . ,” you say, not wanting to ruin it for Jessie with a dose of reality.

But your lukewarm agreement is all the confirmation

Jessie needs. Before you have time to look any more, Jessie grabs your arm. "Come on! Let's follow him!"

Your first experience with a New York City train didn't turn out exactly as you hoped. Okay, that's an understatement. Somehow you got separated from Lena's cousin and squished into a crowded subway car. But since you weren't afraid to ask for help, you got back in touch with Amanda and things seemed like they would work out. But now Jessie's celeb fever has struck again and she wants to go chasing after a guy who may (or may not) be a Jonas brother. You do kind of want to follow him (hey, you never know, right?), but what about Amanda's instructions–are you just going to ignore them? Not sure what you want to do? Let the next quiz clear it up for you.

QUIZ TIME!

Circle your answers and tally up the points at the end.

1. **You have a book report due on Monday. But all weekend they're showing a marathon of your favorite show. What do you do?**
   - **A.** Get out of the house and do all your work in the library so that you can focus on the report.
   - **B.** Stay home, but don't turn on the TV all weekend so that you aren't tempted to tune in.
   - **C.** Work on your report, but give yourself permission to watch an episode or two during your breaks.

D. Watch the whole thing. It's a marathon, for goodness' sake! What kind of sense would it make to watch only an episode or two? You can always ask your teacher for an extension on the report.

2. **Your parents give you an allowance for doing certain chores around the house. What do you do with the money?**

A. You put all of it in a savings account. You might need it for college tuition one day.

B. You put half of it in your savings account and usually spend the other half on school supplies.

C. You put half of it in savings and spend the rest on seeing movies with your friends.

D. Spend all of it on having a good time with your friends. What's the point of working so hard if you don't get to enjoy the rewards?

3. **Your parents go out for a romantic dinner and leave you in charge of your little brother and a handful of chores. What do they find when they get home?**

A. Your homework is done, your brother is safely tucked in bed with freshly brushed teeth, the plants are watered, and the house is spotless. You want them to know they can trust you to hold down the fort while they're gone.

B. Your homework is finished and you've done all your chores, but your little bro is still running around the house like a maniac. He's too much of a handful for you when it comes to going to sleep. Your parents will have to handle that one.

C. You've done part of your homework and one or two of the chores, but when your friend Ericka called, you got distracted and spent the rest of the night on the phone. Can they blame you? She had some serious dirt to spill!

D. Are they home already? You were kind of hoping you'd have another hour or so to relax. When your parents go out is the only time you can get away with blowing off your homework and chores and doing some quality catching up with your DVR.

4. **Your Girl Scout troop has formed a team to participate in a walkathon to raise money for juvenile diabetes. There is a lot to take care of. Your troop leader puts you in charge of:**

A. supervising all your fellow Scouts. You will have to know what everyone's job is so that you can take over if they need help. It's a lot of responsibility, but your leader knows you can handle it. From sending out emails to making sure everyone knows where and when to meet, to helping order the team shirts, you have a hand in everything.

B. keeping a tally of all the numbers and keeping the funds safe. They know they can trust you to keep an eye on all the money raised—and of course not to spend it on yourself!

C. getting the word out to your friends and family. Your job may not carry a ton of weight, but it's important all the same. And with your carefree, fun attitude, you have no problem getting people to support your cause.

D. walking. Someone else has to call you in the morning to make sure you don't oversleep, and you might need a reminder to bring your donations, but walking you can handle, no problem!

5. **Your little sister is going away for a week on a camping trip with her best friend and her family. While she's away, she asks you to take care of her science fair project: growing an African violet, which has very specific care instructions. While your sis is away, you:**

A. follow every instruction to the letter. You keep it away from direct sunlight, feed it a good violet fertilizer, pluck any dead leaves, keep the house a balmy 70 degrees for the best growing conditions, and check the pot's water every two hours once you get home from school. By the time your sister gets back, she is going to have the best-looking African violet in the land!

B. follow most of the instructions, but you get a little lax about plucking the dead leaves and checking the water in the pot every two hours. That part is just going overboard.

C. do what all your other plant-sitting jobs have amounted to: watering it and calling it a day. You doubt you really have to do all that other stuff for the plant to survive. Your sis is just being obsessive.

D. forget all about the plant, and it ends up wilting. Well, how were you supposed to remember? A dog, at least, will bark to remind you that he's hungry or thirsty. The plant never stood a chance.

Give yourself 1 point for every time you answered *A*, 2 points for every **B**, 3 points for every **C**, and 4 points for every *D*.

—If you scored between 5 and 12, go to page 80.

—If you scored between 13 and 20, go to page 72.

chapter FIVE

Hello, Miss Independent! **You feel that you are able to accomplish anything you set your mind to without anyone else's assistance. And you hate admitting it when you can't get there on your own. But you should know that there's no shame in asking for help when you need it. Even the most powerful people in the world sometimes need a hand. (Just ask the president!)**

As the train rumbles along, the knot in your stomach pulls tighter and tighter. You somehow left Amanda back on the platform and you and your two friends are panicking big-time. You're not sure how you got into this mess, but you know you've got to find a way out.

"Lena, why don't you call Amanda?" Jessie asks her.

Lena pulls the phone out of her purse and tries to dial, but nothing happens. "Oh no, I'm not getting any cell reception down here!" she cries, shoving her phone back into her purse in a huff.

"Well, let's ask somebody what to do," Jessie begs.

You glance around at the other passengers, most of whom have headphones on or have their noses buried in books or newspapers. You could ask one of them for advice, but you don't want to look like the clueless tourist you are. "No way. They don't want to be bothered. We're on our own."

The train pulls into the next station and your car empties out enough for Lena to grab a seat. You hope against hope that you'll see Amanda waiting for you, but no such luck.

"Maybe we should get out," Jessie suggests.

"But what if we get out and Amanda is waiting for us at the last stop of this train? If we get out here, we'll miss her," you add.

"But we don't even know where this train stops," Lena says logically. "Some of these trains go to Brooklyn!"

The very thought sends your mind whirling. "Oh jeez . . . What if the train stops in some distant neighborhood and we never find Amanda so we never get back to the bus home and we end up having to drop out of school and live on the streets of New York, wearing fingerless gloves and singing for pocket change?"

Your imagination is totally running away from you.

Thankfully, Lena is there to reel you back in. She stands up and puts her purse down on her seat. Grabbing both your shoulders, she stares deeply into your eyes and yells, "Chill out! Enough with the what-ifs. Here's what we're going to do. We'll get out at the next stop and try to find a signal for my cell phone so that we can call Amanda. Okay?" She glances over at Jessie, who nods weakly, her blond curls looking just slightly deflated.

Finally, after what seems like forever but is probably only five minutes, the train pulls into Forty-second Street and Grand Central Station and you and the girls follow a clump of passengers onto the platform.

The three of you find a pillar to stand behind, getting out of everyone's way.

"All right," you begin, "try calling her now."

Lena nods and reaches for her purse . . . which is no longer on her shoulder. Uh-oh. She looks all around, maybe hoping that she dropped it nearby. But then the realization dawns on all of you: She never picked it up again after she put it on the seat when she got up to calm you down. Her purse is still on the train, which is now rumbling away to the next stop without you.

"Aw, you've got to be kidding me!" Lena yells, watching as the train slips out of sight.

You feel terrible. Lena losing her purse is partially your fault. If you hadn't been spazzing out and refusing to ask for help, she wouldn't have put her purse down. You've got to redeem yourself and save the day. "Hey, guys," you offer, trying to sound confident, "there's a map over there. Maybe we can check it and figure out how to get back to Amanda."

"Couldn't hurt," Jessie agrees, leading the way.

But to you the train map of New York City looks a lot like the pictures of the human blood circulation system in your biology textbook. Only, on the map, there are blue, green, yellow, and even purple veins crisscrossing and curling all over the place. How does anybody ever make heads or tails of it?

Maybe you should speak for yourself, because Jessie seems to be having no problem at all. She finds the You Are Here sign that points at Grand Central and follows the train lines with one manicured fingernail. "Oh, cool!" she says brightly. "Look how close we are to Times Square right now! All we have to do is get on the shuttle train and go one stop and that will leave us in the middle of everything!"

Lena just stares at her incredulously. "Are you crazy? We need to find Amanda and get my purse back!"

"I know, I know," Jessie replies quickly. "And we will. But how cool would it be to go to Times Square first, all on our own? We could run and see MTV Studios real quick, and then call Amanda and try to get your purse back."

You know you can't completely trust Jessie's logic here, because once again her eyes are glazing over with Jonas fever. Lena is clearly not amused. Heading out to Times Square is obviously not the most responsible course of action. But does that mean you shouldn't go? It *would* be pretty exciting. Hmm . . . Both your friends are looking at you to be the tiebreaker.

Is this really happening? Or are you trapped in some kind of nightmare? You chose to leave the safety of your school trip in hopes of having a New York adventure, but this isn't quite what you had in mind. You got separated from Amanda, you have no idea where you're going, and now because you were panicking just a touch (all right, more than a touch), Lena lost her purse on the train. And her cell phone was your only hope of finding Amanda again. You could do the responsible thing and deal with this mess . . . or you could choose to have a little fun first. Which way are you leaning? Take the quiz for the answer—and be honest!

QUIZ TIME!

Circle your answers and tally up the points at the end.

1. **You have a book report due on Monday. But all weekend they're showing a marathon of your favorite show. What do you do?**
   - **A.** Get out of the house and do all your work in the library so that you can focus on the report.
   - **B.** Stay home, but don't turn on the TV all weekend so that you aren't tempted to tune in.
   - **C.** Work on your report, but give yourself permission to watch an episode or two during your breaks.

D. Watch the whole thing. It's a marathon, for goodness' sake! What kind of sense would it make to watch only an episode or two? You can always ask your teacher for an extension on the report.

2. **Your parents give you an allowance for doing certain chores around the house. What do you do with the money?**

A. You put all of it in a savings account. You might need it for college tuition one day.

B. You put half of it in your savings account and usually spend the other half on school supplies.

C. You put half of it in savings and spend the rest on seeing movies with your friends.

D. Spend all of it on having a good time with your friends. What's the point of working so hard if you don't get to enjoy the rewards?

3. **Your parents go out for a romantic dinner and leave you in charge of your little brother and a handful of chores. What do they find when they get home?**

A. Your homework is done, your brother is safely tucked in bed with freshly brushed teeth, the plants are watered, and the house is spotless. You want them to know they can trust you to hold down the fort while they're gone.

B. Your homework is finished and you've done all your chores, but your little bro is still running around the house like a maniac. He's too much of a handful for you when it comes to going to sleep. Your parents will have to handle that one.

C. You've done part of your homework and one or two of the chores, but when your friend Ericka called, you got distracted and spent the rest of the night on the phone. Can they blame you? She had some serious dirt to spill!

D. Are they home already? You were kind of hoping you'd have another hour or so to relax. When your parents go out is the only time you can get away with blowing off your homework and chores and doing some quality catching up with your DVR.

4. **Your Girl Scout troop has formed a team to participate in a walkathon to raise money for juvenile diabetes. There is a lot to take care of. Your troop leader puts you in charge of:**

A. supervising all your fellow Scouts. You will have to know what everyone's job is so that you can take over if they need help. It's a lot of responsibility, but your leader knows you can handle it. From sending out emails to making sure everyone knows where and when to meet, to helping order the team shirts, you have a hand in everything.

B. keeping a tally of all the numbers and keeping the funds safe. They know they can trust you to keep an eye on all the money raised—and of course not to spend it on yourself!

C. getting the word out to your friends and family. Your job may not carry a ton of weight, but it's important all the same. And with your carefree, fun attitude, you have no problem getting people to support your cause.

D. walking. Someone else has to call you in the morning to make sure you don't oversleep, and you might need a reminder to bring your donations, but walking you can handle, no problem!

5. **Your little sister is going away for a week on a camping trip with her best friend and her family. While she's away, she asks you to take care of her science fair project: growing an African violet, which has very specific care instructions. While your sis is away, you:**

A. follow every instruction to the letter. You keep it away from direct sunlight, feed it a good violet fertilizer, pluck any dead leaves, keep the house a balmy 70 degrees for the best growing conditions, and check the pot's water every two hours once you get home from school. By the time your sister gets back, she is going to have the best-looking African violet in the land!

B. follow most of the instructions, but you get a little lax about plucking the dead leaves and checking the water in the pot every two hours. That part is just going overboard.

C. do what all your other plant-sitting jobs have amounted to: watering it and calling it a day. You doubt you really have to do all that other stuff for the plant to survive. Your sis is just being obsessive.

D. forget all about the plant, and it ends up wilting. Well, how were you supposed to remember? A dog, at least, will bark to remind you that he's hungry or thirsty. The plant never stood a chance.

Give yourself 1 point for every time you answered *A*, 2 points for every **B**, 3 points for every **C**, and 4 points for every *D*.

—If you scored between 5 and 12, go to page 89.

—If you scored between 13 and 20, go to page 95.

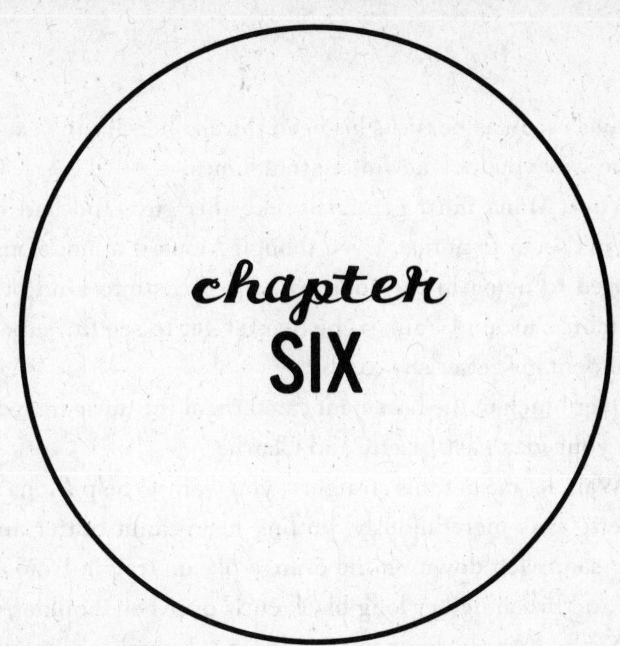

chapter SIX

Congratulations! **You are one of those rare people who are completely able to put themselves in someone else's shoes. When you say that you feel their pain, you really mean it. You hardly ever have serious clashes with others, since you can usually see where they're coming from. And the fact that you always seem to get how your friends feel makes you the automatic go-to person when they need to talk out their problems.**

You can't believe you're going to say this, but you feel bad for Mona. Ever since Amy spilled the beans about Mona's crush on Paul, you've been watching her—from a distance, of course. And you completely recognize the long sideways glances she keeps shooting at him, careful to look away as soon as he turns his head toward her. It's the exact same way you look at Jimmy sometimes.

Wow. Mona must genuinely like this guy. Too bad he doesn't seem to notice. Even though Mona is a model and is used to being in the spotlight, she turns into kind of a dormouse around Paul, so he doesn't get to see the super-confident go-getter she can be.

Over lunch in the basement cafeteria of the museum, you run your idea past Lizette and Charlie.

"Wait, let me get this straight—you want to help Mona?" Lizette asks incredulously, putting her peanut butter and jelly sandwich down on the orange plastic tray in front of her and brushing her long black curls over her shoulder.

"Yeah, I know how it sounds, but I think she really needs—"

"Mona *Winston*?" Charlie interrupts, nervously adjusting his tie. Even on the school trip Charlie is in his usual business attire. His feeling is that there are a lot of business moguls who live in New York—Donald Trump, Diddy, Mayor Bloomberg—and if he should run into any of them, he wants to look the part.

"Yes, all right? You just have to see how she acts around this guy Paul. I bet if she just—"

"Mona Winston, the model from our school who hates you?" Lizette butts in again. "The one who put gum on your seat just because you scuffed her shoe once? That Mona?"

"Yes, yes, yes! Guys, focus, okay? I know she can be a

nightmare. But I just . . . I feel sorry for her. I know how it feels to, um, be in her shoes." You don't have to spell it out for Lizette and Charlie. One quick look over at the far table where Jimmy is sitting with Ms. Darbeau, showing her his sketches, is enough. Your crush on Jimmy is the worst-kept secret in the school.

"Bueno," Lizette mutters softly. "I get it. But what makes you think she would accept your help anyway?"

Good point. If Lena, your most logical friend, were here, she would have asked you the same thing. "I'll think of something."

The Sony Wonder Technology Lab has got to be one of the coolest places you've ever seen. Unlike at the museum, where it was strictly hands-off, you are encouraged to touch and play with everything here. Even the walls light up when you touch them! You wish Jessie and Lena were around to see all this awesome stuff. They both would have flipped over the music-maker exhibit where you get to play with a virtual band. And Jimmy is a pro in their animation studio.

Only when you see Mona milling around the broadcasting booth does a plan finally form in your mind. In the exhibit, kids get to put on their own news show, and everybody has a role. As much as it pains you to admit it, Mona is a natural in front of a camera. She'd make a great news anchor. And Paul is standing right here, so he'd see firsthand what Mona is like at her best.

But since Mona isn't your biggest fan, you'll have to be creative about getting her to participate. You know just what to say.

"Hey, this looks really fun, everybody. Let's do a broadcast. I'll be the news anchor since I'd be *so* great on camera." Scary! You are really channeling Mona's diva 'tude. You start heading for the anchor desk.

"Ha!" Mona chimes in immediately, grabbing the tail of your shirt and pulling you back, just as you expected. "I don't think so. You'd better leave that to the professionals. *I'll* be the news anchor."

You pretend to be really disappointed and settle for the cameraperson job. You may not be as experienced as Mona in front of the camera, but you're not bad with a camcorder. And you're sure you can figure out all these buttons and knobs and make Mona look incredible.

After the staff member gives your group a quick tutoring session on how all this works, he tells you that you can start rolling. You aim the camera at Mona and count down from five, then Mona starts reading a story on the teleprompter about a local recycling program that is really making a difference.

"Until the students of PS two-seventeen got involved, the area around their school was a sea of discarded plastic bottles . . . ," Mona begins, sounding every bit as good as she claimed she would. Now if you could adjust the camera settings so that her image is a little larger and softer . . .

That's what you are going for, anyway. But you end up pressing some button on the side of the camera too hard and it gets jammed. Then every button you press after that just makes it worse. When you look up at the screen, Mona's image, which had looked perfectly normal a second ago, now looks more like a scary fun-house mirror. One of her eyes is huge while the other is barely there, and her mouth is being stretched so wide that she looks kind of like the Joker in *Batman*.

Mona is oblivious to all this until Mark Bukowski points at the screen and shouts, "Check it out, Mona is an alien! Run for your lives!" Everybody starts pointing and laughing—including Paul.

When Mona finally notices what's happening to her image, she turns a deep red and clamps a hand over her mouth. Before you have a chance to scamper away to the girls' bathroom and pretend you were never here, Mona locks eyes with you. Instead of the rage you expect to see on her face, all you find is hurt and embarrassment.

You look around helplessly, really wishing your two best friends were here. But the only person you see not laughing is Jimmy, who is shaking his head at you. "That was pretty mean," he says sadly. Wait, does he think you did that to Mona on purpose? Unbelievable. Your big plan to get Paul to notice Mona worked, all right, but in the worst possible way. Is there a time-machine exhibit in this place? You'd like to go back about fifteen minutes before any of this ever happened, please.

You had good intentions. You did. But they backfired big-time. The plan that was meant to showcase Mona's best side ended up revealing her inner alien instead. She became the butt of everyone's jokes, and Paul had a front-row seat for the whole fiasco. Even worse, Jimmy seems to think you did it on purpose, which isn't cool at all in his book. Can you see a way to fix this mess? Or is running and hiding looking pretty good to you right now? Why don't you start by taking a deep breath . . . and taking the quiz.

QUIZ TIME!

Circle your answers and tally up the points at the end.

1. **Your two best friends have had a huge fight and haven't been on speaking terms for days. What should you do?**
   - **A.** Stay out of it! People who step between two friends in a fight only end up getting hit by the crossfire. No, thanks. For now you'll try to avoid being around either of them and hope the whole thing blows over soon.
   - **B.** Talk to each of them individually about the rift and how it's affecting you. Hopefully that will inspire one (or both) of them to break the silence and fix things already.
   - **C.** Invite them both over to your house for a study session (without telling either of them that the other friend will be there, of course). They might be mad at you at first for

tricking them, but you're sure once they're in the same room at the same time, they'll end up working out their differences. The three of you can never stay mad at one another for long.

D. Call for an emergency friendship meeting, inviting them to air out their problems while you listen to both sides and weigh in. No one leaves the room—not even to use the bathroom!—until the issue is resolved. This silent-treatment business has gone on long enough. It's time to take action so that you can all get back to normal!

2. **You are about to head out to a friend's birthday party when you realize that you totally spaced and forgot to get him a present. So naturally you:**

A. skip the party. It's too late to get anything now, and no way can you show up empty-handed. You'd rather not be there at all than to have to explain how you could be such an airhead and forget to get him a gift.

B. go to the party but leave right before the opening of the presents. Maybe no one will notice that none of the boxes on the gift table are from you.

C. tell the birthday boy that you ordered his gift online and it just hasn't arrived yet. That's not entirely true (okay, that's not even partially true), but it'll buy you some time.

D. give him something of yours that means a lot to you and that he's always admired, like your autographed copy of the very first Harry Potter book, or the framed photograph of the two of you hanging upside down on the monkey bars on your first day of second grade. And you can make him a card on your computer. You don't have to spend a dime to show your friend how much he means to you.

3. **This afternoon is your first movie date with your longtime crush. But this morning you woke up with a zit in the middle of your forehead that is big enough to have its own zip code! What do you do?**

A. Cancel the date and reschedule for next week. With any luck, by then you'll look a little less like a meteor landed on your face.

B. Tell him you'll meet him inside the theater after the movie has started—and you'll have to take off before it ends. The key is to be in complete darkness the whole time so that there's zero chance of him catching a glimpse of the hideous intruder living on your dome.

C. Wear a bandanna around your forehead, covering the offensive pimple. No, a bandanna isn't your usual style, and it doesn't go with your outfit in the slightest, but desperate times call for desperate measures!

D. Go on the date, forehead volcano and all, and even crack a joke or two about it. If he's cool, he'll totally understand and look past it. After all, who hasn't dealt with the occasional visit from the acne fairy?

4. **You and your buds are in your living room practicing your dance moves for the upcoming recital when you accidentally kick over**

your mom's favorite lamp and send it crashing to the floor. Now what?

A. Make tracks! If you aren't home when your mom discovers the damage, she can't pin it on you, right?

B. Clean up the mess, throwing the evidence away in a nearby Dumpster. When your mom asks what happened to the lamp, you try your best to convince her she never had a lamp like that and you don't know what she's talking about. Better for her to think she's losing her mind than for you to get in trouble!

C. Try your best to glue the lamp back together. Sure, it's missing several chunks and now looks more like a science experiment gone horribly wrong than a lamp, but maybe your mom won't notice?

D. Fess up to what happened and offer to buy a new lamp using your allowance. No use trying to hide it.

5. **You have bitten off more than you can chew at school and now you have a report due, a play to star in, and a track meet to preside over as captain all in the same week. It would be almost impossible to do it all, which means you'll have to:**

A. fake being sick and not do any of them. The thought of even trying to accomplish all the things on your to-do list this week is just too overwhelming. If you don't show up, you're sure the play and track meet will go on without you. And you guess you'll have to take an Incomplete on the report. Not ideal, but better than facing all the chaos.

B. do the report, but bail on the play and the track meet. You'll be putting the drama club and track team in a bind and they'll be mad, but facing the fury of your parents if you fail to hand in your report would be way worse. Everyone else will have to deal.

C. try to do all three. Most likely your team will lose the track meet since you haven't had time to motivate them; you'll fumble your way through the play since you haven't memorized all your lines; and your report will def be less than stellar. But at least you will have tried.

D. decide to delegate. You hand your star part over to the understudy (who is psyched) and opt for a less demanding role in the chorus; assign the best runner on your team to be cocaptain so that she can pick up the slack until you're back on your A game; and enlist the help of your folks to help you research your report. Where there's a will, there's a way!

Give yourself 1 point for every time you answered **A**, 2 points for every **B**, 3 points for every **C**, and 4 points for every **D**.

—If you scored between 5 and 12, go to page 108.

—If you scored between 13 and 20, go to page 104.

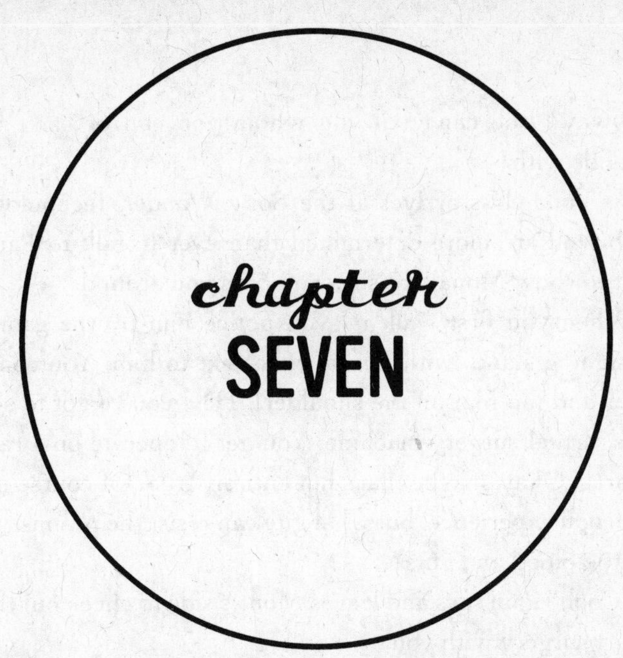

chapter SEVEN

Other people are a real mystery to **you, even your closest friends and family. You don't always understand what makes them tick, and you have a tough time identifying with anyone's experiences but your own. The secret to it is that, as different as people are, they all experience the same feelings. How you would feel in a given situation probably isn't much different from how another person might feel. You just have to practice putting yourself in their shoes—even if you don't think they'll fit you.**

You just don't get Mona. You're so sick of her taking her bad moods out on you. Amy claims she's acting that way because she secretly has a crush on Paul. But you doubt it. From what you can tell, the only person Mona cares about is Mona. Who does she think she is, anyway? She can't tell you whom you can or can't be friends with!

As your class arrives at the Sony Wonder Technology Lab, you are more determined than ever to talk to Paul, just to show Mona that she can't boss you around.

When you first walk in, you notice him by the game-designing stand, with Mona right next to him. You come over and tap him on the shoulder. "Hey, you've got to see this virtual surgery machine. You get to operate on a real heart!" Okay, maybe that's not entirely true. Of course it's a virtual experience, but what guy can resist the promise of a little blood and guts?

"Cool," Paul says and leaves Mona's side to check out the heart surgery with you.

But he isn't there for even ten minutes before Mona comes back and swears up and down that Paul's teacher is looking for him over at the nanotechnology exhibit. Paul drops his scalpel midsurgery and heads away with Mona, who turns around to smile an evil little smile at you.

That's how it goes the whole time you're in the lab. You barely even talk to Jimmy, Lizette, or Charlie because you and Mona are caught in a game of tug-of-war over Paul. How you got sucked into this, you're not quite sure. You only know that you're determined to win.

Rockefeller Center in December is unreal. There are two lines of angels in white facing one another, blowing brass trumpets into the air. Giant snowflakes made of light are spinning on the buildings surrounding the ice-skating rink. Watching over the skaters is an enormous gold statue in front of a running waterfall. And towering over everything is a Christmas tree that must be a million feet tall with about two million twinkling lights in every color you can imagine hanging from its branches.

Unfortunately, you're too busy looking at Mona to appreciate the amazing view around you. Paul was the first to lace up his ice skates and get out there. (According to your teachers, you'll be here for only forty-five minutes, so you've got to make the most of your time.) You're in a race to lace up your ice skates before Mona does. But Mona seems to be some kind of ice-skate-lace expert. She sits on a bench across from you and giggles as you struggle to untangle the laces and shove your foot inside, then never even looks down as she quickly undoes her own laces, slips her tiny feet into the skates, and crisscrosses the laces with a speed that matches Mark's hot dog–eating abilities. She's that fast. She heads out onto the ice, probably loving the slack-jawed look on your face.

"How did she do that?" you wonder out loud.

"Easy," Amy answers, taking a seat on the bench beside you. "Mona used to take ice-skating lessons when she was little. Her mom thought they would help her modeling career. You know, to learn poise and stuff?"

You shrug.

"Anyway," Amy continues, "she took lessons for years, so she probably learned all the tricks the pros use."

"As usual, you're full of helpful information, Amy," you respond listlessly, not even bothering to question how she knows all this.

Amy shakes her head happily. "I try!"

Great. So now the tug-of-war is going to take place on Mona's turf. You inhale a couple deep breaths of cool December air, trying to psych yourself up.

"Are you ready?"

At first you think the voice is coming from your own mind. But then you look up and see Jimmy wobbling unsteadily on a pair of tan skates. He's holding both his arms out to balance himself and you can already tell that he won't last long on the ice. Not upright, anyway. It's pretty adorable.

"Sure," you answer. "Let's go."

Since you're actually a decent ice-skater, you lead Jimmy out onto the ice, letting him hold on to your arm until he starts to feel more at ease. But even then, he's skating with his knees bent and his toes pointing at each other, pushing forward in short little bursts.

"Hey, I think you're getting better!" you shout encouragingly.

"Liar," Jimmy says, clutching your arm even tighter.

You laugh. "All right, so you skate like I paint. We each have something we're good at, and that's why we make such a good team."

Jimmy gives you a warm smile and nods his head, and for a second there you don't even notice that it's about forty degrees outside. But then you see his eyes shift away from your face and go wide. "Whoa! Where'd she learn to do that?"

You turn just in time to see Mona doing a fancy camel spin, then a sit spin, as tourists lining the rink whip out their cameras to take pictures. But she doesn't seem to care at all about the crowd. After each trick, she looks around to see if Paul is watching, which he is. She does a final spin where she leans back, raises one leg behind her, and then lifts her arms in graceful arcs so that it looks like an oval is framing her head. "Not bad," you mumble grudgingly.

"Not bad? She's incredible!" Jimmy exclaims, his eyes gleaming in a way that you hoped was reserved only for you.

Just then, Mona comes swerving by and whispers quickly in your ear, "Top that, rookie."

If that isn't a direct challenge, you don't know what is.

Even though you're in New York, New York, things between you and Mona are the same old, same old. As usual, you've managed to get on her bad side just by existing. But this time you've refused to take her bossy mind games lying down. Paul unknowingly became the rope in a game of tug-of-war between you and your nemesis. And after those Olympic-style moves on the ice, it looks like Mona's going to win his attention after all. But the real victory would be if she succeeded in making you feel insecure. Will you fall into the trap? You know what your mind says, but how about your body? Take the quiz for a quick gut check.

QUIZ TIME!

Circle your answers and tally up the points at the end.

1. **You are walking past a group of mean girls at school and right after you pass, they burst out laughing. What do you think they found so funny?**

   A. They are obviously laughing at you. You probably have TP stuck to your shoe, or maybe they're laughing at the skirt you're wearing. You knew you should have gone with the tights and ballerina flats. Maybe you can find a locker to hide out in for the rest of the day. . . .

   B. They might be laughing at you, but they could be laughing at any of the dozens of kids pacing the halls too. You aren't the only one on their geek radar.

   C. Who knows? If they are laughing at you, you'll take it as a compliment that they're trying so hard to make you feel self-conscious. They only do that to girls they consider threats.

   D. Who cares? You have way more important things to focus on than a group of mean-girl wannabes. You actually have a life.

2. **You notice that a lot of your favorite stars are going under the knife and getting plastic surgery. Is that something you would consider when you get older?**

   A. In a heartbeat! You have a laundry list of things you would fix if you could. A ton of surgeries might do the trick.

B. Well, maybe you would have a few things done. You wouldn't go overboard, but you'd be lying if you said there weren't at least three things you'd love to change.

C. Only if you had a real medical problem, like a broken nose or webbed feet, or if one of your legs was shorter than the other. Anything else would be a little too sci-fi for your taste.

D. Not a chance! You're happy with the way you look, flaws and all. Why anyone would go to such extremes to end up looking like a plastic doll is beyond you.

3. **As a homework assignment, your English teacher had you each write a poem about your life, and now she's asking for volunteers to stand up and share what they wrote. You:**

A. will yourself to become a chameleon and blend in with your chair. What you wrote is personal and you don't want your classmates judging you while you read. What if they think it's lame?

B. don't volunteer, but resign yourself to reading your poem to the class if your teacher picks you. You just hope someone else wrote a really long poem that'll take up the whole class period.

C. wait until a few other people volunteer so that you can see the kind of stuff the other kids wrote. If they bare their souls first, maybe you'll feel secure enough to bare yours.

D. are the first to volunteer. Your life is an open book and you don't mind letting your classmates in on it. Plus, you don't think your poem is half bad.

4. **A new girl, Chloe, just transferred into your class and everyone seems to think she's really smart, super-nice, and pretty. You react by:**

A. starting some crazy rumor about her to tarnish her perfect rep. Anyone that perfect makes you all look bad. You're doing everyone else a favor, as far as you're concerned.

B. making sure you're assigned to the same team for the group projects. That way you can get to know her in a neutral setting and find out what her secret flaw is. Nobody can be that perfect!

C. giving her a chance. You aren't immediately on Team Chloe, but if she really is as nice and smart as everyone says, maybe she'll be worth getting to know.

D. becoming her friend immediately! She sounds like a cool person (actually, she sounds a lot like you!) and you know you'll get along really well.

5. **A guy you've started spending time with has finally added you as a friend on Facebook. When you start checking out his page, you see that he has hundreds of friends—and a lot of them are pretty girls. You feel:**

A. like defriending him right away. Obviously he is interested in these other girls, and adding you to his Facebook page was just his way of telling you.

B. a little insecure. With all these cool people in his life, could he really be interested in you?

C. flattered that he has included you in his world. It's clearly a popular place to be, so you must have made the grade.

D. that he's pretty lucky to know you. He may have a ton of cool-looking Facebook friends, but you know there's no one quite like you, who can keep up with him in the classroom and make him laugh so hard that milk spurts out of his nose. You definitely bring something special to the table.

Give yourself 1 point for every time you answered **A**, 2 points for every **B**, 3 points for every **C**, and 4 points for every **D**.

—If you scored between 5 and 12, go to page 115.

—If you scored between 13 and 20, go to page 123.

Tsk, tsk, tsk. **You love to have fun and are sometimes considered the life of the party. But you aren't the most responsible girl in the world. Without realizing it, you could be building a reputation as someone who can't be depended upon, so you are likely to get passed over for some great opportunities (like summer jobs), and it might take you longer to earn freedoms from your parents that they think you would abuse. Show that you can be responsible when you need to be, and you will end up getting more freedom as a result.**

You know you should probably stay right where you are, but what if that really is Nick Jonas walking down the sidewalk? If Jessie has Jonas fever, you must have caught it, because you find yourself yelling "Let's go!" and taking off after Jessie down the block.

"Guys, no! What are you doing?" Lena shouts behind you. But you hear her footsteps take off after yours.

"He . . . went . . . this way!" Jessie yells over her shoulder, panting but never dropping her pace. As you run, a woman walking a tiny Chihuahua wanders into your path, and you have to hurdle the dog as if it were one of those road cones in gym class. Then Might-Be-Nick crosses the next huge avenue just before the light changes for Jessie. The three of you watch helplessly as he gets to the other side of the huge intersection and sticks one arm into the air.

Seconds later, a yellow cab swoops into place in front of him and he climbs in. When the traffic light changes, the taxi comes barreling past you and your friends. You can see the figure you've been chasing sitting in the backseat without his sunglasses on, and . . .

It isn't Nick Jonas. It's just a regular guy—who actually doesn't even look like Nick once you see his face. You can't say you're surprised. What in the world would make you think a Jonas brother would be walking around with zero security following him, anyway?

Jessie's shoulders slump in disappointment. "I could've sworn . . ." She doesn't have the heart to finish.

You pat her shoulder comfortingly. "I thought so too, Jess. But hey, if you want, we can tell Amy what happened, and by the time she spreads the word, the story will be that we chased the *real* Nick Jonas down the street!"

Jessie smiles at the thought.

"Or I could tell her that the two of you spent the whole

day trying to get us killed," Lena says. "What were you guys thinking? I almost got flattened by a bike messenger back there!"

You wince. "Sorry, Lena. I guess we weren't thinking. But this will be the last time we go chasing after a celeb, cross my heart." You make an X over your heart with your index finger.

"Unless it really *is* him next time," Jessie adds. "In which case, all bets are off."

Lena fights the smile creeping onto her face. She can never stay mad at you and Jessie for long. "What am I gonna do with you two?"

"Well, the smart thing would be to stay far, far away from us so that you don't catch Jonas fever too. It seems to be contagious. But for now, let's just go back to where we were, and try to meet up with your cousin."

Lena nods, adjusting the strap on her purse. "Good idea. Let's go."

As the three of you round the corner, heading back to the train station exit where you first called Amanda, you are all smiles . . . until you spot the flashing red and yellow lights. Uh-oh.

As you get closer, you see a frantic-looking Amanda standing with her back to you as she talks to a police officer. "They're all thirteen years old, Officer, and Lena—that's my cousin—is wearing a black puffy coat and white scarf, jeans, and white sneakers. . . ."

"Kind of like the girl behind you is wearing?" the officer asks politely.

Amanda whirls around and spots the three of you approaching. Her eyes go from wide with panic to awash with relief. "Oh, thank God!" She runs to Lena, squeezes her in a tight hug, and then touches your head and Jessie's, inspecting you as if she's looking for war wounds. "Are you girls all right? I was worried sick! When you weren't here when I got here, I figured something serious must have happened for you to leave this spot, so I flagged down this police car. Did someone bother you? What happened?"

You and Jessie exchange nervous glances. In the face of the police car lights—and Amanda's frantic eyes—chasing down a Nick Jonas look-alike now seems downright crazy. But if you tell Amanda the truth, she may just have the officer toss you into the back of his squad car and haul you off to jail anyway. Decisions, decisions . . .

You are your own worst enemy. You could have had a pleasant day touring New York with your class (including your crush, Jimmy), but nooo. . . . You wanted to have an adventure in the city. Unfortunately, that started off with you getting lost on the subway and losing Amanda. Luckily you got back in touch with Lena's cousin, and that could have been the end of it. But nooo. . . . You had to go running off to chase down what turned out to not even be Nick Jonas. And because you did that,

Amanda panicked and brought in the police, and they want the truth. You could deliver that . . . or maybe you could dream up something better? Only the quiz can predict what you'll do now.

QUIZ TIME!

Circle your answers and tally up the points at the end.

1. **Your favorite kind of movies are ones that:**

   A. take place in entirely different worlds, like *Alice in Wonderland* and *Avatar*. It's cool to see the most far-out things a person can imagine.

   B. take place in the real world but have some kind of supernatural element, like the *Twilight* movies. You like imagining that something like that could actually happen to you.

   C. have a science fiction theme, like *Iron Man 2*. With the right technology, anything's possible!

   D. are set in average neighborhoods and are about typical kids. To you it's way more interesting to see how people deal with the real world.

2. **If you had to choose what you're going to be when you get older, you'd choose to be:**

   A. something creative, like an artist, fiction writer, or choreographer—anything where you'd get to let your imagination run wild.

   B. a kindergarten teacher. You'd like to be the one to spark the imagination of little kids and see what they come up with.

C. a historian. The true stories of the past are so much stranger and more entertaining than anything you could make up!

D. an accountant. You love dealing with numbers and facts. The totals are either right or they're wrong.

3. **When you go to school each day, your friends know they can count on you to:**

A. look completely different every time. New hairdo, new outfit, whole new vibe. You like challenging yourself to see how many different looks you can create using your wardrobe.

B. look a little different whenever they see you. You have some basic looks you rely on, but you like throwing something different into the mix too—like combining a couple of your old lip glosses to make a brand-new color, or changing up your hairstyle.

C. look the same almost every day, but on your birthday or picture day you like to wear something special. (Finally, a chance to wear that sequined top!)

D. look exactly the same week in and week out. You're kind of like one of those cartoon characters that rocks the same outfit every day, or close to it. What else is there besides jeans and T-shirts?

4. **Your parents have taken you and your little sis on what was supposed to be a luxury vacation, but when you get to the hotel, you find out that the website completely misrepresented the place. Not**

only is it not luxurious, it's kind of a dump. How do you handle the unfortunate turn of events?

A. You take it in stride. Where other kids might see a dump, you see a chance to stretch your imagination. You picture the pitiful fountain out front as an Olympic-size pool. And that cold breakfast of stale muffins and warm OJ? A feast for a king with all your favorite foods! Pretty soon your sis is playing along and you all make the best of it.

B. You are kind of disappointed, but for your parents' sake you convince yourself it's way better than it is.

C. You're bummed, but you'll spend most of your time reading anyway. If you can't be somewhere fabulous, you can at least read about somewhere fabulous.

D. You complain loudly and beg to go home. You can't picture having a good time here at all.

5. **When you dream, you tend to dream:**

A. in full, vivid color! And your dreams tend to be about far-off places you've never been and feature people and creatures you've never met. Most of your dreams are like crazy little movies!

B. pretty weird things. (Like that time you dreamed you had toothbrushes for hands? Weird!) But usually, even the weird things are taking place in your regular school or in your house.

C. kind of boring dreams that aren't much different from your real life. You have lots of dreams about your friends or schoolwork. (Your dreams might make other people sleepy!)

D. . . . who knows? You never remember your dreams, if you have any at all.

Give yourself 1 point for every time you answered **A**, 2 points for every **B**, 3 points for every **C**, and 4 points for every **D**.

—If you scored between 5 and 12, go to page 131.

—If you scored between 13 and 20, go to page 141.

chapter NINE

You are the poster child for responsibility. Parents trust you to babysit, teachers seek you out as an assistant, and friends know they can depend on you to bring them their homework assignments when they're sick. You never blow off things you've committed to and you're just all-around dependable. If only you could rub off on everyone around you!

"Hold it right there, missy," you say to Jessie, sounding a little like Lena when she's trying to rein you in. You grip the back of her jacket and stop her from moving even an inch farther. "We're not going anywhere until Amanda gets here."

"But—but . . . ," Jessie stammers. "What if that really *is* Nick Jonas?"

"So what if it is? Did you notice how fast he was moving? Looks like he doesn't want to be bothered right now anyway. Plus, if Amanda comes and we're not here, she might call our parents and then we'll all be grounded for life. Is an autograph worth it?" Lena nods approvingly at you. Her common sense was bound to rub off on you eventually.

Jessie breathes out heavily, casting a wistful glance back at the figure in the black coat, who turns a corner and is gone. "No, I guess not. But if anybody asks, can we at least tell them we think we saw him?"

"Deal," you say, grabbing her hand and swinging it up and down in an exaggerated handshake, making her giggle and temporarily forget about her near-Jonas experience.

At last Amanda sweeps out of the train station, looking even more harried than she did this morning. "Oh, thank goodness!" she exclaims as she hugs all three of you. "Thank you for being so smart and getting off at the next stop to call me. I was worried you would stay on the train and end up in Brooklyn!" She chucks Lena under the chin with one hand and winks at you. "I should have known you girls could handle yourselves in the big bad city."

At Amanda's words, you fill up with pride. She's right! New York has tested you and you passed. But it's even cooler to hear that from someone older like Amanda, who actually lives here.

"So you're not mad?" you ask a little nervously.

"Mad? Why would I be? I did nearly have a heart attack when I saw those doors closing. But getting pushed onto the train was an accident. Could have happened to anyone. What's important is that you guys were smart and you followed directions. If I were on *The Amazing Race,* I'd choose any one of you as a teammate in a heartbeat."

You instantly picture you and Amanda racing through Manhattan with huge backpacks on, searching for a clue together in front of the Empire State Building. You suddenly wish Amanda were your cousin too.

"And since we're here now, that kind of decides where we're going next."

"Where to?" you ask enthusiastically.

"You'll see," she answers in a singsong voice, grinning happily.

Even the outside of F.A.O. Schwarz looks like something out of a picture book. A guard dressed as a toy soldier stands at attention outside the store, his patent leather hat and boots polished to a shine. You think in passing that he'd be pretty cute if not for the giant red circles painted on his cheeks.

As you follow Amanda one at a time through the revolving doors, you are greeted by a huge clock that reaches the ceiling and happy music welcoming you to their world of toys. Everywhere you look are rows and rows of realistic-looking stuffed animals, some tiny enough to fit in your pocket, others too big to even fit in your bedroom.

"What is this place?" Jessie asks, staring around in wonder.

"Only the best toy store in the world," Amanda gushes. "I know it was before your time, but have any of you seen the movie *Big* starring Tom Hanks?"

You and Lena both raise your hands. Lena once spent a rainy weekend at your house, where the two of you watched half the movies in your mom's DVD collection, and *Big* was your favorite. You especially loved the scene where the main character and his boss play the giant piano on the floor.

"Well, that was filmed right here," Amanda continues. "There's even a picture from the movie upstairs near the floor piano."

"Wait, you mean the piano is actually here?" you ask incredulously. For some reason, you'd thought that was just movie magic.

"Sure is. Come on, I'll show you."

As you follow Amanda through the maze of dolls and Lego buildings, you think if this is New York, you could definitely live here.

Before you know it, you arrive in a wide hallway where a few people are buzzing around, stepping gingerly on a huge mat that looks like a piano keyboard. Above it is a still frame of your favorite scene from the movie. "Awesome," Jessie says next to you. "We're on an actual movie set!" She starts looking around as if she expects celebrities to start pouring from the aisles.

After the tourists who got there before you move on, Amanda is the first to step onto the keys. "Okay, which one of you knows how to play 'Chopsticks'?"

Lena smiles and takes one hesitant step forward, but you can't contain your excitement anymore. "I do! I do!" you shout and leap into position. Together, you and Amanda jump around the keyboard, playing the song in perfect time. A crowd begins to gather, some of them snapping pictures. When you're done, everyone claps. Amanda clasps your hand, raises it above your head, and then swings down in a deep bow. "Thank you, thank you!" she shouts. "We'll be here all week!"

As you head back downstairs on the escalator, you nudge Lena. "Oh my God, wasn't that awesome? Amanda is a riot."

"Yep. Awesome," Lena says in a clipped voice, seeming to look everywhere but at you.

Today could have turned into a giant disaster. After you got swept onto the train and separated from Amanda, anything could have happened! But because you asked for help and then waited for Amanda to come get you, things are finally back on track. You and Lena's cousin are hitting it off famously. And speaking of famous, you got to reenact one of your favorite movie scenes of all time! So far, everything is perfect . . . at least, you think so. But could there be something you're

missing? Take the quiz to see if you notice anything outside your happy little bubble of fun.

QUIZ TIME!

Circle your answers and tally up the points at the end.

1. **You've come down with a terrible case of tonsillitis—which unfortunately for you means that you were unable to audition for the play this afternoon (something you had really been looking forward to). When your best friend comes by to tell you how well her audition went, how do you respond?**

   A. "That's awesome! Tell me all about it, every single detail!" You know how exciting it must have been for your bestie. You would never rain on her parade by focusing on yourself.

   B. "Great. I'm glad it went well for you." It still stings that you weren't able to audition, so it doesn't exactly feel good to hear about anyone else's experience. But this isn't just anyone. This is your best friend, so you try your best to put on a brave face and be happy for her.

   C. "Cool. Did anyone ask about me?" You're glad your BFF got to audition, but what you really want to know is how everyone else took your absence. Surely you were missed!

   D. You cut her off before she even has a chance to say anything. "Don't even tell me about the audition! I've been lying here all day feeling miserable. Let me tell you all about the gross medicine I had to take. . . ." What you've been dealing with all day is way more dramatic than any play. Your bud's going to want to hear all the gory details.

2. **You just got back from several weeks of being away at camp. At long last, you run into your friends from school that you haven't seen all summer. What's the first thing you do?**

   A. Ask them about everything you missed in their lives. Did Jen ever get up the nerve to talk to that cute lifeguard at the pool? Did Lydia pass the AP bio class she took? Did Tommy save up enough from his dog-walking job to buy the new PSP game he had his eye on? Inquiring minds want to know!

   B. Let them fill you in on everything they've been up to, and then tell them the biggest thing that happened to you at camp. Becoming a camp counselor is big-time! The rest of the details you can catch them up on later.

   C. Spend an hour going back and forth with your friends, each one of you offering up one new piece of information at a time before hashing it out and moving on to the next bit of news. It's the power catch-up.

   D. Tell them all about your time at camp in excruciating detail. Your summer was crazy exciting and you know they're going to want to feel like they were right there with you.

3. **When it comes to Twitter, you:**

   A. check out everyone's tweets, even celebrities and people you don't know. It's fun to see what other people are up to.

B. see if anyone responded to your most recent tweet. You put your opinion out there about your school giving the afterschool program the ax, and you're dying to see if anyone agrees.

C. check out your friends' tweets—especially the ones that have to do with you. (Those are usually the ones that crack you up the most.)

D. read over all your own past tweets. They're so funny when you read them all together like this. You should write a book!

4. **You just found out that Sarah, the star of your debate team, will be dropping out of the competition because of a family emergency, and this is right before the semifinals. Everyone is pretty shaken up by the news. What is your first thought?**

A. *Sarah loves the debate team and she wouldn't drop out before semifinals unless something pretty important came up. Maybe we should all leave the competition so that we have more time to rally around her and offer our support.*

B. *I really hope she's okay. Our team will have to work even harder now to make her proud.*

C. *Oh no! That's terrible for Sarah, but what about the team? I hope we can still do all right without her.*

D. *Why do bad things always happen to me? Now we're one member short! But . . . does that mean there's an opening for a new star of the team? That could be me!*

5. **You go on a fun school trip to a nearby farm and when you get home, you download all the pics to your computer. What did you take pictures of?**

A. All your pictures are of the scenery—the cows, the pigs, the acres of cornfields—all the stuff you don't see every day.

B. Most of them are of your friends. The one of your best friend trying to get the goat to stop eating her sock is hilarious!

C. You managed to get your teacher and the farmhands to take a bunch of you and your friends. You love having photographic evidence of all the good times you've had together.

D. All the pictures are of you. You plan to put these up on Facebook for your family to see, so you should be in every shot, right? Thank goodness for the timer function!

Give yourself 1 point for every time you answered **A**, 2 points for every **B**, 3 points for every **C**, and 4 points for every **D**.

—If you scored between 5 and 12, go to page 156.
—If you scored between 13 and 20, go to page 146.

chapter TEN

You are the poster child for responsibility. Parents trust you to babysit, teachers seek you out as an assistant, and friends know they can depend on you to bring them their homework assignments when they're sick. You never blow off things you've committed to and you're just all-around dependable. If only you could rub off on everyone around you!

As much as you would love to see Times Square, you vote with Lena.

"Sorry, Jessie, but Lena's right. We really need to try to find Amanda and hopefully get Lena's purse back. You get that, don't you?"

Jessie sighs miserably and shrugs. "Yeah, I get it. I just hate it when you guys are right."

"Yeah, the sooner you accept the fact that I'm always right, the happier you'll be," you joke, patting Jessie on the back. "Now, how do we get out of here?"

"Just a hunch," Lena says, sounding a bit calmer, "but I'm guessing we follow the Exit signs."

"Good hunch," you agree. "Let's go."

You climb a few sets of stairs, turn through a few hallways, and eventually end up in a ginormous room packed with people going every which way. There are arches leading to railroad tracks, rows of ticket booths, and a giant clock centered between two sides of a grand staircase. And at the top of the stairs—daylight! Bingo.

You and your friends weave through the commuters rushing to catch trains and tourists stopping to take pictures, and climb the stairs until you find yourselves standing on a busy New York street. Phew!

"Okay, we're outside. Now what?"

"Well," you say, taking a moment to think, "I guess the first thing would be to find your phone, Lena, since we need it to call Amanda. So how about I call your number to see if maybe somebody picked up your purse on the subway and turned it in?"

"It's worth a try," Lena says sullenly, clearly not having much faith in the plan.

"Hey, cheer up," you say, pulling out your own phone.

"We'll find Amanda and you'll be quoting Shakespeare again in no time."

You hit the speed-dial button for Lena and bite your lip, hoping with all your might that somebody, anybody, answers. What you are completely unprepared for is the voice that actually does answer.

"Hello? Lena, is that you?" a quavery-voiced Amanda asks on the other line.

"Amanda?" you screech, surprised into a whole other octave of your voice.

Lena, who had been staring at her shoes, shoots her head up and her mouth drops open.

You quickly press the speakerphone option so that you can all hear. "Yes, it's me!" Amanda shouts. "Tell Lena a really nice woman found her purse on the train."

"Sweet!" Jessie exclaims. "But how did you end up with her phone? That's some magic trick."

"No magic necessary," Amanda answers. "With Lena's mom's help, I was able to have her calls forwarded to me in case you called. And you did! Where are you guys?"

After you walk down to the nearest corner and read Amanda the street signs, she tells you to stay put and she'll be right there after she picks up Lena's purse. "I have a surprise for you three that I think you're going to like."

Amanda gets to you in record time, and even though you just met her today, seeing her familiar face among the crowd of strangers feels almost as good as seeing your own parents after a long stay at summer camp. She, in turn, hugs each one of you as if you've been separated for days instead of under an hour.

"First things first," she says after you finish celebrating your reunion. "Are you guys hungry?"

"Starving!" you shout in unison. Not until she asked did you even realize how much.

You are finishing your second slice of pizza at a nearby pizzeria when Lena finally asks, "I don't mean to rush you but, um, are you ever going to tell us what this surprise is?"

Amanda dabs her mouth with a paper napkin and smiles happily at you all. "Yep," she says. "I just wanted to make sure I told you the news when you had full stomachs so that you wouldn't pass out on me or something."

"News worth passing out over?" Jessie pipes up. "Sounds promising!"

"Well," Amanda begins, "when those doors closed in my face, the first thing I did was try to call Lena, but of course I had no cell reception. So I went upstairs and tried again a little while later. The first few times I called, it went straight to voice mail. But on the fourth try, someone answered."

"Fourth time's the charm, huh?" you say.

"In this case, it sure was! It turns out a woman who was on the train with you saw you get off and leave Lena's purse behind. She picked it up, intending to turn it in. But when she heard the phone ring, she answered and we ended up talking. We arranged a meeting place and I had your calls forwarded. Then I met up with her and she gave me your purse back, Lena." Amanda nods to her cousin. "It all happened so quickly. When I explained to her what had happened, and how you three were spending your first time in New York City lost on the train, she felt sorry for you. Turns out she works at MTV and was given a bunch of passes to something to give to clients. But she decided you guys needed them more."

With that, Amanda hands Lena a sealed envelope. Lena slides one finger under the flap and swipes it across in one smooth motion, then pulls out four hard pieces of cardboard that must be some kind of mirage.

"Are these . . . ?" Jessie asks, afraid to even finish the question in case her eyes are deceiving her.

"Yep," Amanda answers nonchalantly. "Four passes to the dress rehearsal of Nick Jonas's concert." Amanda shrugs, pretending to be bored. "I don't know if you even know this Nick Jonas person. You don't have to go if you don't want."

"Are you freaking kidding me?" Jessie yelps, practically leaping across the table to hug Amanda. "Of course we want. We want!"

You look around the pizzeria with an embarrassed grin, noticing all the other patrons staring at your table. "Sorry, everybody," you say. "She was raised by wolves."

"Whatever," Jessie yells, "I don't care. I'm a wolf girl who's going to see Nick Jonas today! Aaaaooooh!"

Everyone who told you New York could be unpredictable sure was right! There's no way you could have foreseen getting separated from Lena's cousin and having to navigate the subway system on your own. You also didn't know how well you three would handle it, or that you'd cross paths with such a Good Samaritan on the train. And here you had heard that all New Yorkers were mean and rude. Clearly that isn't true. Thanks to one extremely kind person—and the very cool Amanda, of course—Lena got her purse back and you all scored tickets to a private Nick Jonas concert rehearsal. If the city is always this exciting, you can see why it never sleeps!

QUIZ TIME!

No quiz necessary this time. All aboard to page 161! Next stop: Nick Jonas concert!

chapter ELEVEN

Tsk, tsk, tsk. You love to have fun and are sometimes considered the life of the party. But you aren't the most responsible girl in the world. Without realizing it, you could be building a reputation as someone who can't be depended upon, so you are likely to get passed over for some great opportunities (like summer jobs), and it might take you longer to earn freedoms from your parents that they think you would abuse. Show that you can be responsible when you need to be, and you will end up getting more freedom as a result.

You should absolutely, positively, without a doubt *not* go to Times Square instead of tracking down Lena's purse and reconnecting with Amanda. Yep, that's what your brain is telling you. But your feet seem to have other ideas.

They're already walking in the direction of the small gray

S signs directing you to the shuttle train while you plead with Lena. "We'll find Amanda again, I promise. But think how much fun it will be to see Times Square completely on our own first!"

"Not much fun without my purse!" Lena points out. "Have you both lost your minds?" You can see that Lena is getting more agitated by the second, and isn't loving the fact that you and Jessie have outvoted her for the sake of some crazy desire to see the bright lights of Broadway sans adult supervision.

"Lena," you say earnestly, "who knows when we'll get the chance to come back here? This could be our one opportunity to have our own little adventure in New York City! How cool would it be to tell all the kids at school that while they were on the school trip being forced to walk in two straight lines, we were off in Times Square by ourselves, seeing the sights? I mean, just for a minute," you add hastily.

As responsible as Lena is, you can see that shell start to crack and the idea of having a little independent fun begin to take hold.

"Well, maybe just for a minute . . ."

"Good call!" Jessie says, grabbing her hand and racing through the wide-open hallway leading to the S train lines. For a train that goes only one stop, it sure is crowded. The three of you huddle around a shiny metal pole as a voice comes on over the intercom telling everyone to stand clear of the closing doors. There's the now-familiar ding followed by the whoosh of the doors sliding shut, and you're off!

* * *

You pull into the Times Square stop about two minutes later and follow everyone else out into the station. Even without any signs at all, you would guess that you were in Times Square. Everywhere you look is a sign for a different train line, and there are at least half a dozen exits. People are zooming by in every conceivable direction. And above the hum of all that is the steady beat of hip-hop music and the sound of clapping hands.

As you move closer to the screens on the wall broadcasting a basketball game, you see that just in front of them is a group of five or six men in white T-shirts and baggy jeans doing a choreographed dance right there in the subway station. This place really is like living in a musical. People seem to be breaking into song and dance all over the place.

You step up to join the line of people watching and see one man using an empty paint bucket to add to the drumbeat already pouring out of the speakers from the radio on the floor. "Ladies and gentlemen," the front man announces, "don't be shy. Clap your hands!" He gets them started by clapping his own hands high above his head, and a few people up front start to join in. Without even realizing it, you have started to groove along to the music, clapping and swaying and trying to copy their complicated moves.

Finally the one in front points at you and says, "Hey, you in the green hat, get up here, girl! You can dance!"

You look to the left and to the right of you, but you're the only one wearing a green hat. They mean you!

"Go for it," Jessie squeals. "Show 'em how it's done!"

You step forward and two of the group members stand on either side of you, running you through a few of their simpler moves. When they think you've got it, the front man announces you're going to take it from the top. He counts off and the whole group of you runs through the routine, and you're holding your own. As you dance you can see the crowd growing bigger and bigger. You even remember the hand movements and totally land the pose at the end, after which everyone watching starts applauding like crazy, Jessie and Lena loudest of all.

"If you liked what you just saw," the front man yells, "feel free to give anything you can so we can keep this going." The man who was playing the overturned paint bucket turns it right side up and moves through the crowd collecting change and dollar bills. Once the crowd starts to disperse, the front man claps you on the back and says, "Great job! You can get down with us anytime."

You smile from ear to ear. "Thanks, that was so cool."

"Not as cool as the amount we just collected," the drummer says behind you. "You really helped us draw a crowd."

"As a matter of fact," the front man says, reaching into the bucket and counting out a number of bills, "this is your share. Thanks for being a good sport."

Your eyes bug out of your head. "Really?"

"Really," he confirms. "Go out and buy your friends something nice."

"That was fabtastic!" Jessie yells as you ride the escalator up to the street level. "We're walking around with a professional dancer now!"

"Aw, it was nothing," you say modestly, unable to stop smiling.

But one thing that is definitely *not* nothing is the view awaiting you outside the train station. The bright lights of Broadway is right! Every inch of this place is lit up with neon lights and eight-story billboards for Broadway shows and clothing lines. Vendors are set up all along the sidewalk selling roasted peanuts, pretzels, hot dogs, and glossy black-and-white photos of New York. The streetlamps are all decorated with red and green garlands and the shop windows have decorations in them celebrating all the different holidays.

You buy your friends warm salty pretzels with your professional dance earnings and saunter down the busy sidewalk feeling amazing. When you come to one of your favorite clothing stores, you wave Jessie and Lena inside and buy three I ♥ NEW YORK T-shirts so you'll all have a memento of your day in the city. You're about to leave when the salesperson informs you that everyone who buys something gets to have their picture taken together and have it displayed on a huge screen outside.

"Just show us where to stand," Jessie says with a cheesy grin. The three of you do your best Tyra pose as the photographer snaps the picture. They even let you add a line underneath it.

The three of you leave the store glowing, each with a

waxy shopping bag, a half-eaten pretzel, and what Kara DioGuardi would call swag. You're laughing and joking around as you leave the store, aiming straight for MTV Studios in hopes of seeing a certain Jonas brother, until you bump right into the decidedly not smiling Amanda.

"Having fun?" she asks sarcastically.

That's a trick question. Don't answer that.

"Um, yes?" D'oh! What part of "don't answer that" didn't you understand?

"Oh, you are?" Amanda says, planting her hands on her hips. "Because I haven't been having any fun. I have been pulling my hair out looking for the three of you!"

"Amanda!" Lena exclaims, belatedly realizing you've all been busted. "How did you find us?"

"It wasn't easy," she says. "First I went upstairs to call Lena's phone, but no one ever answered. So I got back on the train and got off at the next stop, thinking you three might do the same, but you were nowhere to be found. I asked every station agent I saw, but no one remembered seeing you. So finally I got scared enough to call your parents," Amanda says seriously, looking at you and Jess.

"You called my mom and dad?" Jessie asks, all the glee that was in her voice earlier entirely gone.

"Yes. Good thing too. Your mom told me you have a tendency to wander off, which is why she had a GPS chip installed in your phone."

The shock on Jessie's face tells you this is news to her.

Jessie pulls out her phone and stares at it as if she has had a secret spy with her all along.

Amanda purses her lips, clearly trying to hold in her anger. "So I had them track you and they told me you were in Times Square. And then I got a phone call from someone who found Lena's purse on the train."

Lena's mouth drops open. "Someone found my purse?"

"Yes, and lucky for you, it was found by someone who was willing to return it. I told the woman I'd come get you first and then we'd go by her office and pick up the purse. But did you not even notice it was missing? Or didn't you care?"

"I can explain," Lena says miserably. "I mean, it wasn't like we just came here to have a great time or anything."

"Oh, really?" Amanda says, nodding. "Because I wasn't sure exactly where you were in Times Square until I saw that."

She points above your heads, so you all turn around and see a giant snapshot of you, Jessie, and Lena with the words "Having a great time in Times Square!" underneath it. Oh wow . . . you guys managed to bust yourselves!

"I'm so sorry," Jessie is the first to say. "It was all my idea. Lena didn't even want to come."

"Yes, well, Lena should have known better than to follow along. I mean, I love New York, but any major city can be dangerous. And all of your parents trusted me to keep you safe!"

By now, all three of you are having trouble making eye contact with Amanda. It's been a long time since you felt like you were in this much hot water. But you feel even worse that you dragged Lena into it.

"Just tell me this," Amanda continues, finally seeming to lose some of the edge in her voice. "What were you thinking?"

You shrug. "I don't know. I guess we just wanted to have fun and feel glamorous and maybe see a star or two. That's what New York is all about, right?"

Even to your own ears, that sounds a little shallow. By the way Amanda is shaking her head, she thinks so too. Then she nods slowly, as if she has made some kind of decision. "You know what? You three are going to be in plenty of trouble when you get home, so I won't make you feel any worse. But I do think I need to show you what's really important. First we'll go pick up Lena's purse. Let's go."

Amanda must not want to risk losing you on the train again, because she sticks out her arm to hail a yellow cab. You all climb in, prepared to take any punishment she has in mind. You're pretty sure you deserve it.

It seems like every turn you made today was the wrong one. You decided to leave the school trip and go see the sights with your friends.

But instead you ended up getting pushed onto a speeding train and getting lost in the subway system. Instead of asking for help, you freaked out, ultimately leading to Lena losing her purse on the train. You could have salvaged the day right then and there by calling Lena's parents right away so they could call Amanda, but instead you chose to have a grand old time in Times Square on your own. That part was pretty fun, but was it worth all the trouble you're now in with your parents and with Amanda? Probably not. Let's just hope Amanda isn't planning something for you that would make spending the day with Mona Winston feel like a picnic.

QUIZ TIME!

No getting out of this one. Just go straight to page 167 and prepare for a lesson in humility.

chapter TWELVE

You're a problem solver. When things go wrong, you don't panic, you don't sit around and whine, and you definitely don't run away. Instead you try to come up with a way to fix them. You live by the motto "If you're not part of the solution, you're part of the problem." As long as you're aware that there will be some things even you can't fix, it's never a bad idea to at least try.

What just happened? All you wanted to do was help. So how did you end up humiliating Mona instead? It's been a few minutes and the other kids are still gathered around the broadcast studio monitors laughing at Mona's hideously warped face, made all the worse by her furious blushing. This was not what you intended at all. Time to do some quick thinking.

In your experience (mostly from embarrassing things that have happened in the school cafeteria), the easiest way to get kids to stop laughing at someone is to get them to laugh at something—or someone—else. In this case, the someone else will have to be you. Without hesitating, you come out from behind the malfunctioning camera and step right in front of its lens. Suddenly Mona's fun-house face is replaced with your own—and yours looks even worse since you're so close to the camera. "Hey, everybody," you call, "Mona's idea for an all-alien newscast is awesome. Look, I'm an alien too. Take me to your leader!" You pull the sides of your mouth open with your index fingers and stick your tongue out like a lizard. The effect on the monitor is both horrifying and hilarious. From this angle, your forehead is the size of a watermelon, your eyes look like golf balls, and your lizard tongue looks like a tiny finger is poking out of your nose.

"Ugh, gross!" Mark grimaces. "Do me next!"

"My pleasure." You get back behind the camera and point it at Mark, who is instantly transformed into a creature that is a cross between a zombie and duck-billed platypus.

"Cool!" Mark says, really hamming it up. But he doesn't get even fifteen seconds of fame since everyone starts clamoring to be next in the freak show, including Paul and Jimmy. Before long everyone has taken a turn and is laughing about how sick you all looked, even Mona.

"But did you see the size of my ears?" Shawna asks.

"Yeah. Dumbo would have been jealous!" Dionne answers.

"Hey, you guys don't see an eyeball on my neck, do you?" a redhead wearing a pair of thick glasses asks them, stretching her neck.

Dionne makes a show of really searching for the eyeball. "Nah, your neck is eyeball free." And they all burst into laughter.

Hearing the uproar, a technician finally shows up and "fixes" the camera, and all the kids move on to other exhibits. Only when no one is looking do you approach Mona and say, very softly, "Sorry, that was an accident."

"I know," she says simply.

"Hey, Mona," Paul calls from across the room. "The IT guy said he might have all our faces on tape. Let's go watch it again. That was too funny!"

"Be right there!" Mona calls back. And without looking you in the eye, she mutters, "Thanks," and trots over to Paul.

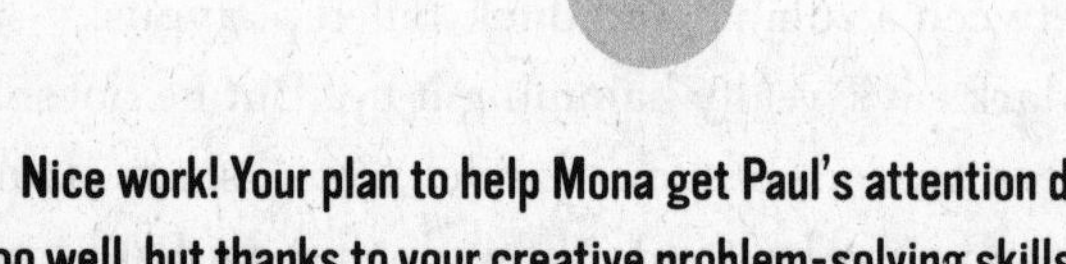

Nice work! Your plan to help Mona get Paul's attention didn't work out too well, but thanks to your creative problem-solving skills, you came up with something even better! Not only did you get the whole class cracking up, you got Paul to see Mona as someone with a wicked sense of

humor. Whether that's actually true or not, he'll find out in time. But at least Mona saw firsthand that if she lightens up a little, people might actually enjoy her company. And would being friends with you somewhere down the road be completely out of the question? Well, don't push it. But hey, if there are aliens in New York City, anything is possible. Until then, you've got one more stop on the itinerary before you have to call it a day. Hope it's a good one!

QUIZ TIME!

Sorry, but it's almost time to head back home, so there's only one choice from here. Go to page 172 and see what Ms. Darbeau has planned for your big finale.

chapter THIRTEEN

When problems come knocking, your first response is to lock them out and barricade the door. The flaw in that plan is that you have to come out eventually, and when you do, the problems will still be there waiting for you. If you practice coping with your problems instead of avoiding them, you'll find that you get better and better at it over time. Roadblocks that used to seem like big mountains will start to look more like puny anthills.

If you had been trying to play a cruel joke on Mona, you would not have come up with anything this effective. All the kids—from your school and the New York school—are literally pointing and laughing at her, to her obvious horror. It's like a scene out of a Lifetime movie about bullies or something. Even Paul is joining in, which is not at all what you were hoping for. You wanted him to pay Mona some attention, but not like this.

You wish you could take it back, but you're too stunned to even say anything, and from the shell-shocked look on Mona's face, you doubt she'd be open to an apology from you anyway. The best you can do is go get the Sony technician and have him fix the camera, which he does. But the damage is done. Before the technician came, Amy Choi, always one to capitalize on moments like this, took a picture of Mona's mangled face with her new smartphone and posted it on her Facebook page. The awful pic is making the rounds like lightning and it's all your fault.

But the icing on the cake is that Jimmy can barely stand to look at you. You would hope that he knows you well enough by now to know that you would never do something so mean, not even to Mona, who—let's face it—sometimes asks for it. But just when you approach Jimmy to try to explain what happened, Jasmine Viera comes up and claps you on the back. "Oh my gosh, that was genius!" Jasmine trills. Then she leans in and stage-whispers, "Don't tell Mona I said this, but she really had that coming. Good job!"

Groan. *So* not what you wanted Jimmy to hear. And it's not even true. But Jimmy turns away, shaking his head. Except for Lizette and Charlie, no one believes it was an accident. When you finally catch a glimpse of Mona scampering away to the ladies' room, there are tears in her eyes.

"Any chance you think she'll just forgive and forget?" you ask Lizette and Charlie.

"Well, I could get out my calculator and quantify the exact probability of that happening for you," Charlie offers, "but if I had to ballpark it? I'd say slim to none."

Fantastic. Thanks to your own handiwork, the rest of your big exciting day in New York City is going to achieve a whole new level of lame. And just when you thought you couldn't feel any worse, your cell phone vibrates in your pocket, letting you know you just got a text message. It's from Jessie. You open the message to see a picture of her, Lena, and Amanda standing in the middle of Toys 'R' Us. There's an enormous Ferris wheel behind them and they're each holding up a rainbow-colored swirling lollipop. The message reads: Wish u were here!

Yeah, you wish you were there too.

You hoped that by the time the class reached the next stop on Ms. Darbeau's itinerary, the incident at Sony Wonder Technology Lab would be nothing but a distant memory and you'd be feeling way better. But so far, no such luck.

If anything, you've just turned into a big ball of paranoia. Mona is kind of the "don't get mad, get even" type, so you've been waiting for her to get back at you ever since. When you boarded the bus, you double- and triple-checked your seat for gum—Mona's favorite weapon of choice. When you got off the bus in front of the Rockefeller Center ice-skating rink, you kept watching your back to see if any stray snowballs were flying toward your head. And now that you're here, looking onto the ice, which is full of happy-looking kids and couples, all you can picture is Mona tripping you up so that you fall flat on your face. Maybe you are overreacting, but like the T-shirts say, just because you're paranoid doesn't mean they're not out to get you.

Rather than take the chance, you refuse to go out there, leaving Mona to own the rink. Even the obviously popular crew from the New York school—a group of brunette girls rocking matching black puffy coats and slicked-back ponytails—clears the way for Mona every time she glides by. Between the Lab and here, she has managed to pull herself together and insist that the incident at the broadcasting booth was her idea. Some kids believe her and some don't, but the few that do allow her to show her face in public. Still, you're pretty sure you catch a hint of sadness in her eye whenever she glances at Paul, who has gone back to ignoring her, more or less. It's clear to everyone that what she said about Paul worshiping her just isn't the truth.

You could say the same for Jimmy re: you. Since you and Jimmy started becoming friends, you've felt so in sync with him. You've never had a fight and you were sure you'd always be on the same page. But now look at him. All the way over on the other side of the rink, talking to everyone but you. For archenemies, you and Mona sure have a lot in common.

You're sitting there thinking about the irony of that situation when Paul comes skating over to the bench where you're hiding out. "Hey, Picasso girl. You ever planning on putting on your skates? This is an ice-skating rink, you know." He smiles at you and rubs his two gloved hands together.

"Nah, I don't think so," you reply, trying to keep the whine out of your voice. "I'm not sure I'd be too welcome out there." You steal a glance at Mona, who's making her way around the rink with an ease that says she's taken lessons before.

Paul notices your glance. "What, you mean Mona? I wouldn't worry about her. You seem pretty nice, so if you pulled a joke like that on her, she probably had it coming. Even the kids in my class think so, and most of them don't even know her."

"What? No! The whole thing was an accident. I would never do something like that to anyone, not even someone who hates me. And anyway, aren't you a friend of hers?"

Paul shrugs. "Well, even though she was always kind of a spoiled brat, we were friends when we lived next door to each other. But she's been so weird around me all day."

"Do you really not know why?" you press. Are boys really that dense?

Paul just tilts his head in confusion.

"Maybe I shouldn't be the one to tell you this, but . . . Well, Mona doesn't like many people, but I think she likes you. She told everyone in our class about you and seemed psyched to see you again—"

Realization washes over Paul's face and he winces. "Until I acted like a big fat jerk and helped make fun of her at the Lab," he finishes for you.

"You said it, I didn't." You shrug.

"Like I said before," Paul says, "you really know your stuff." Ah, if only you felt like that was true!

"Will you excuse me?" Paul says suddenly, checking to see where Mona is now. "I think I need to go catch up with an old friend."

With that, he skates across the ice and joins Mona, even holding out his arm for her to latch on to. You see Paul lean over and say something to her and she whips her head to look right at you. You could be wrong, but you swear that her eyes soften and the corner of her mouth lifts into an almost smile. Whatever Paul said to her may have gotten you off the hook. But you're still staying off the ice—just in case.

It's been a weird day. Your two best friends bailed on you to go have fun in the city, you and Jimmy had your first falling-out, and you found yourself actually trying to help Mona, who has never exactly chosen you to share a best-friends charm with. On top of that, your classmates have mistaken you for the type to play mean jokes on people, and Mona's secret crush somehow became the key to your redemption with her. Weird, weird, weird. But now that your day in New York is drawing to a

close, hopefully some things will get back to normal. You'd settle for just one, though. (Hint: His favorite artist is Picasso.)

QUIZ TIME!

You've done all you can do at this point. All that's left is to go to Ms. Darbeau's final destination on page 172 and hope that the spirit of the season takes over.

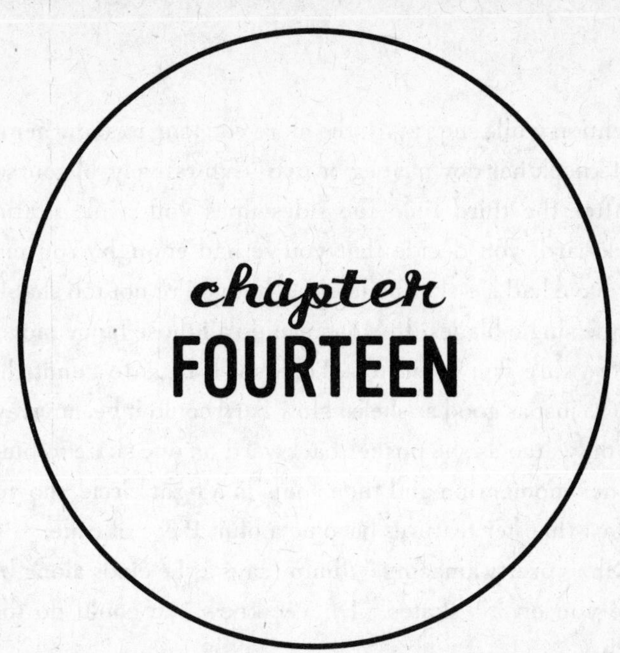

chapter FOURTEEN

You go to great lengths to prove to everyone else that you're special. However, if you were truly secure in that knowledge, the only one you'd feel the need to prove it to is yourself. There will always be someone out there who you think is smarter, prettier, or more talented than you are. But if you learn to accept your shortcomings and embrace your strengths—everyone has both—you'll feel less insecure and no one will be able to shake your self-confidence.

Mona has some nerve. She is determined to make you feel bad about yourself with her snide little remarks and gleefully evil looks. The worst part? It's totally working. The longer you sit on the sidelines watching her skate circles around everyone else in the rink (and getting Jimmy's attention while she's at it), the more you long to show her up and knock her down a peg or two—figuratively, of course.

After the third time she sideswipes you while skating backward, you decide that you've had enough. You may not have had ice-skating lessons, but you're not too shabby on the single blades. If Mona can do all those fancy moves, you're sure you could too. Then she'll have to admit that you're just as good as she is. How hard could it be, anyway?

You watch as she pushes backward on one skate to build up her momentum and then spins in a tight circle, moving so fast that her features become a blur. Piece of cake.

"She's pretty amazing," Jimmy says as he clods along beside you on his skates. "I never knew she could do that trick."

The admiration in his voice is just too much for you to take. "What, that?" you say, trying your hardest to seem unimpressed. "That's no big deal at all. Watch."

You deposit Jimmy back on the side of the rink so that he can grip the wall while you show him how it's done. You've watched plenty of ice-skating and it seems easy enough. Just as Mona had done, you push back on one skate, holding your arms out for balance and bending your knees as you glide backward. Then you angle your right foot as you move into a slow spin. You've got it! Well, you've kind of got it. Um, actually, maybe you don't got it at all. Your ankle tilts in a way you're pretty sure it isn't supposed to, and you go crashing to the ice, your ego crashing right along with you.

As you lie there waiting for your head to stop spinning (and your backside to stop throbbing), the other kids on the rink have to skate in a huge circle around you to avoid running you over. Too bad the ice is frozen solid. At this moment, you wouldn't mind if it cracked and sucked you under, you're so embarrassed.

"Hey, are you all right?" Jimmy asks as he holds out his hand to help you up. You let him pull you slowly to your feet.

"Uh, yeah," you answer sarcastically. "I did that on purpose. Wasn't it cool? I call it the double ankle twist."

"Impressive," Jimmy says, letting you lean all your weight on him as he leads you off the ice. "I give it a nine point four."

After he sits you down on the first bench you reach, Jimmy tells you he'll be right back. "I've got to find a staff member. Maybe they'll have an ice pack for your ankle, to stop the swelling."

"Ironic," you mumble. "The ice *caused* the swelling too."

Jimmy grins and walks clumsily away toward the skate-rental booth. As soon as he turns his back, the full horror of what just happened hits you. You tried to compete with Mona on the ice and ended up totally humiliating yourself. You can't believe you fell! You wouldn't be at all surprised if your Rock Center wipeout made Amy Choi's YouTube Hall of Shame, right alongside Lena hurling into a trash can at the mall and Mark butchering a Disney classic during his choir audition. Ugh. Turns out Mona *is* better than you at something. Much better. And now you've got the swollen ankle to prove it.

You lean over, rest your elbows on your thighs, and clamp your hands over your face, trying to give yourself a pep talk. *Maybe Mona didn't even see me fall,* you reason. *And maybe Paul was busy getting hot chocolate or having his picture taken in front of the huge golden statue, so he missed it too. Maybe—*

"Smooth moves out there." Mona's voice cuts through your inner monologue.

"Get lost, Mona," you say, not bothering to come out from behind your hands.

"Well, I should expect that kind of behavior from you," Mona says mockingly, as if she's appalled by your rudeness. "That's probably why Paul wants to hang with me and not you," she continues.

At that, you finally lift your head. You may be down right now, but you're certainly not out. "You wish," you say hotly. "Paul has been talking to me all day and you can't stand it that he can't stand you."

Mona flinches involuntarily, perhaps because what you said hit too close to home. "That's not even true," she protests. "He's into me."

"Not even," you shoot back. "He'd rather hang with me."

"Me."

"Me."

This back-and-forth is quickly descending into a Celia-and-Delia-style argument. (Lizette's twin cousins go at it like this all the time.)

But before you have a chance to go any further, Paul

comes striding over with a girl you recognize as one of the New York students.

"Hey, Picasso girl," he says. "Are you all right? I saw you hit the ice out there. Looked pretty nasty."

Mona smiles smugly.

"Yeah, I'm fine," you say, trying to sound as if you actually are. "It was nothing."

"All right," he says with a one-shoulder shrug. "Glad you're okay." Then he glances at the petite blonde next to him, whose baby blue hat, scarf, and gloves all match her eyes. The bridge of her nose is sprinkled with a cluster of light brown freckles that look as if a professional makeup artist placed them there. Slipping an arm around her shoulder, making her giggle happily, Paul says, "Janine and I were just about to go get some hot chocolate. Either of you want one?"

You look over at Mona, who looks back at you, grim realization and shock registering on both your faces. "No, thanks," you say in unison.

Paul gives you another half shrug. "Suit yourselves," he says. "Come on, Janine. Maybe they'll have those little marshmallows you like."

They turn away and leave you and Mona looking at each other in utter confusion. It's as if you were both *American Idol* front-runners who got eliminated in the same night.

"So . . . neither one of us?" Mona says in genuine shock.

You slump. "Guess not."

"But that means I spent this whole trip fighting over—"

"Absolutely nothing," you finish for her. "It was pretty boneheaded of us to go this psycho anyway. There were way cooler things to do in the museum and the Sony Lab than obsess over some boy."

"Agreed," Mona says quietly. "I'm not even sure I liked him anyway. Maybe I just miss New York."

It is a stunning confession from Mona. This might be the pain in your ankle talking, but if someone didn't know better, they'd think you and Mona were friends.

Just as you have that thought, Mona clears her throat, shakes out her lustrous black hair, and stands up. "And if you tell anyone that we had that Hallmark moment, I'll deny it and make you wish you'd never been born."

"Naturally," you answer. Now, that's the Mona you're used to.

Before she has a chance to strut away, you hear an announcement blasting over the rink's sound system.

"And now, ladies and gentlemen, please clear the ice to welcome our surprise guest, Nick Jonas!"

No. Way. You had to have heard that wrong.

But the paparazzi that have suddenly sprung up all around the rink tell you that your ears were not playing tricks on you. You watch as Nick steps out onto a small platform at the end of the rink that wasn't there a minute ago. "Thanks, everybody. As you know, I'm going on tour soon to promote my new solo album. The first concert will be right here in New York City!" The crowd goes wild at this news, clapping and whistling, while camera flashes pop all around Nick. "I'm just here to give four concert tickets and backstage passes to one lucky fan."

What? Where is Jessie when you need her? She should totally be here for this.

"We chose this person at random just a few minutes ago as we were watching everyone skate. So let's have the lucky winner come on up!" Nick shouts. "The passes are yours!"

You watch in total disbelief as one half of the gloom-and-doom duo from your school, Holly Deever (aka Holly Happy-Go-Lucky), goes gliding up to the stage in her entirely black outfit and stringy brown hair to accept the tickets from Nick. Her best friend, Mary McCullen (better known as Mary Sunshine), claps half-heartedly and smirks as if this is all so very boring. "How do you feel?" a reporter asks Holly cheerfully, shoving a mike in her face. "Are you excited?"

Holly nods. "Yeah, it's all right, I guess."

You tune out the rest of Holly's gloomy acceptance and Nick's obvious discomfort. (You're sure he's much more used to fans going a little crazy when they're near him.) All you can think about is the fact that had you not been so focused on outshining Mona for the sake of a boy, you would have been on the ice when they were choosing a fan to give the tickets to, and that might have been you up there instead of Holly. Lesson *so* learned.

Jimmy finally returns with a staff member, who applies a cold compress to your ankle and wraps it with a beige ACE bandage, telling you the swelling should go down soon and you'll be fine. Too bad there's no first-aid kit for bruised egos.

What came over you today? You didn't think you were the type to fight with anyone over a boy or to allow insecurity to make you do something foolish. But that's exactly what you did. As a result, Paul ended up choosing someone else altogether to hang out with, you missed out on what could have been a fun day with Jimmy, you had an epic fall on the ice and twisted your ankle, and (most devastating) your preoccupation with one-upping Mona left you out of the running for some backstage passes to the Nick Jonas concert. The only bright spot was the sincere moment you had with Mona, but even that was short-lived. Overall, it just hasn't been your day. But you do have one more stop on the itinerary. Hopefully it'll be kind to you.

QUIZ TIME!

Sorry, but from here all roads lead to one place. Let's hope this last bite of the Big Apple is sweet. Go to page 172.

chapter FIFTEEN

Congrats! You are one secure young lady. You may not be the best at everything, but you believe in yourself enough to try, and you actually enjoy your own company. Because you really know who you are, others would have a hard time making you feel inferior. Your happiness with yourself means you don't feel the need to put others down or get caught up in petty fights. This is a valuable trait. Hold on to it!

Watching Mona try so hard to get Paul's attention makes you realize how utterly ridiculous you've been. You don't need to prove anything to her, and you definitely don't need to make a fool of yourself over some boy—a boy you barely know anyway.

"Come on, Jimmy," you say, ignoring Mona's taunts. "Let's see if we can get you up to speed on these skates."

"Speed?" Jimmy asks nervously. "I don't like the sound of that. How about we just get me up to a slow crawl? That I think I could do."

You giggle happily. "Oh, come on. You're not that bad. I bet in no time you'll be—"

Your sentence is abruptly interrupted when Jimmy's left foot slips out in front of him and the two of you go tumbling down in a heap. "You were saying?" Jimmy says sheepishly, his dark green eyes twinkling. And you both start laughing. Fighting off the giggles, you stand up, pull Jimmy to his feet, and try again. By the time you make it around the rink just once, you've fallen no less than four times, each spill funnier than the one before it. He does start to get the hang of it, though, and before long he doesn't need to clamp on to your arm for support—although he does hold on to it anyway as a gentle snow begins to fall. (If Jess and Lena were here, they'd be giving you a big thumbs-up right now.)

You can't even believe you wasted a minute on Mona drama. For the first time today, you are really having fun.

You are rounding a bend with Jimmy when you see a news camera on the side of the rink, and two brunette women waving you over. One of them extends her hand for you to shake. "Hi, I'm Tara Tallan, a reporter for Channel Nine News. You two look like you're having fun out there," she says.

"Definitely!" you agree, knowing your excitement is all over your face.

"Are you from New York, or is this your first time here?" the woman standing next to Tara asks.

"First time," you respond. "And so far, it rocks."

The two women smile and nod at each other, seeming to decide something. "Well," the second woman starts, "your day is about to rock even more. Do you happen to be a fan of Nick Jonas?"

Is she kidding? Of course you are. If you weren't, Jessie might defriend you on Facebook or something. "Without a doubt," you answer confidently.

"Good." The woman nods. "And what if I told you that I had four tickets and backstage passes for you to attend his concert next week?"

Your heart starts beating a little faster at the very thought. "I'd say are you for real?"—hoping very much that the answer is yes.

"I am," she says, smiling broadly. Finally she extends her hand. "My name is Sarah Little and I'm one of Nick's representatives. As you may have heard, he's in New York right now promoting his new album, and we've arranged for him to do a surprise drop-in at the rink today to give one lucky fan these backstage passes." She holds up a sealed envelope. "We used to have him pick the winner, but that has caused near riots in the past, so now we do it a little more quietly and just have him come in at the end for a brief photo op."

You're having trouble processing what Sarah is saying. You suddenly feel like you might be sleepwalking. "Uh . . . are you trying to tell me that you're giving me these passes? And that I'll be meeting Nick Jonas?"

"That's what I'm saying," Sarah confirms, blinking a snowflake out of her long brown lashes. "Just make sure you don't leave the ice. Nick will be here in a second, but we can't stay long."

OMG!!! This is the part where you freak out so much that Jimmy presses his hands over either side of his head to protect his eardrums from your high-pitched squeals of delight. You can't even believe your luck! "Yes, yes, YES!" you scream. And across the rink, you suddenly hear, "No, oh no, owww!"

Looking behind you, you see Mona sprawled out on the ice, grabbing her ankle. You may have been ignoring her, but Mona was still putting on quite a show for Paul, pulling out all the stops. It seems that her last camel spin was one too many and she went flying.

"Come on," Jimmy urges you. "Let's go pick her up and take her to get help. She's going to need ice on that." He starts heading over toward Mona, but turns back when he realizes you aren't following him.

"Um, are you crazy?" you ask bluntly. "Didn't you hear what Sarah said? Nick Jonas is going to be here any second. *Nick Jonas*. And I have to be here to accept those passes."

Jimmy looks stunned. "But she could be really hurt."

"Sorry, Jimmy," you say, shaking your head. "But I . . . I don't want to miss this."

"Oh." He blinks rapidly, as if he's had something in his eye for hours and is just now seeing clearly. "I thought you were . . . Oh, never mind." He shakes his head and turns back toward Mona, who is still planted on her behind, rubbing her ankle. Everything was great a few minutes ago, and you scored some dream tickets, which is good. So why does it suddenly feel so bad?

Will your issues with Mona never cease? So far she's ordered you not to talk to Paul, taunted you on the ice, and somehow, without even trying, altered Jimmy's opinion of you, making your Nick Jonas tickets win a little less sweet. But if you're honest with yourself, you'll admit that it takes two to tango and it wasn't all Mona's fault. Right now she is legitimately hurt and you actually refused to help. It will take more than mere words to redeem yourself for that in Jimmy's eyes and in your own. But how much are you really willing to sacrifice? You may think you know, but take the quiz to see if you're right.

QUIZ TIME!

Circle your answers and tally up the points at the end.

1. **It's your thirteenth birthday and you're psyched! Your favorite part is:**

A. the presents! You can't wait to rip into some shiny wrapped packages with your name on 'em.

B. getting to say that you're officially a teenager. Finally you get to join the club! You can't help feeling special.

C. having a good excuse to throw a party and show your friends a good time. It really wouldn't matter whose birthday it was—getting to go to the roller rink and laugh your heads off would be a riot no matter what!

D. seeing your friends' faces when they open their goody bags. (They're going to love the rubber-ducky key chain that quacks when you squeeze it.)

2. **As you were walking past the new salon in the mall, one of the workers handed you a few coupons for free services as part of their Grand Opening promotion. Sweet! What are you going to do with them?**

A. Use them all, of course! It isn't often that you get your nails done by a professional. You'll use one to get a manicure, one for a pedicure, and maybe you'll get a shampoo while you're at it. . . .

B. Save them so that you can bring your friends with you. It'll be more fun if you can all get manicures together.

C. Use one for yourself and give the other two to your mom for her birthday. She could use a little pampering at the salon.

D. Give all the coupons to the charity Dress for Success, which helps low-income women prepare for job interviews. It's a great cause and now you can contribute!

3. **When your friends sleep over at your house, you always:**

A. take your bed and let them curl up in sleeping bags on the floor. It would take a lot more than a slumber party to make you give up your supercomfy mattress.

B. let one friend join you in the bed, but the rest will have to take the floor. It's only fair—when you sleep over at their houses, you're on floor duty.

C. invite everybody to pile onto your bed. If you all sleep sideways, you just might fit. And it'll be easier to whisper your ghost stories if they're all close by.

D. take a spot on the floor alongside your friends. Part of the fun of a slumber party is feeling like you're camping out in the woods or something. You'll leave the bed free for anyone who decides the floor is too uncomfortable.

4. **You and the cutie from your history class are both doing a report on the California gold rush. You get to the library at the same time and find out that there's only one copy left of the book you both need. So of course you:**

A. race through the history section to get to it first and check it out before he even has a chance to lay his eyes on it. He may be cute, but you're fast!

B. make sure you get to the book first, then tell him you'll lend it to him when you're done. (It'll probably be a while, though.)

C. tell him the two of you can share the book. You are looking for the same info, after all. (Plus, spending the day rubbing elbows with a cutie won't exactly be torture.)

D. let him have the book. You're way better at researching on the Internet than he is, so he'll need the book more than you will anyway.

5. **You and your little sister have let your rooms become total disaster areas. Your parents tell you both to clean up, and whoever finishes first will win a little extra money in her allowance this week. Who comes out on top?**

A. You do. You are older, faster, and a little more in need of extra allowance. Your sister will just have to work harder next time!

B. You finish first, but you give your sister a little bit of the reward money so that she can buy herself a consolation prize.

C. You finish first, but then go over to your sister's room and help her finish cleaning. You split the money with her. You both earned it.

D. You are a pro at cleaning your room and could have done it in minutes flat, but you take your sweet time so that your little sis will win. You know that she's saving up to buy a bike and has been working really hard. So now she'll have a new bike and a clean room to put it in!

Give yourself 1 point for every time you answered **A**, 2 points for every **B**, 3 points for every **C**, and 4 points for every **D**.

—If you scored between 5 and 12, go to page 182.

—If you scored between 13 and 20, go to page 176.

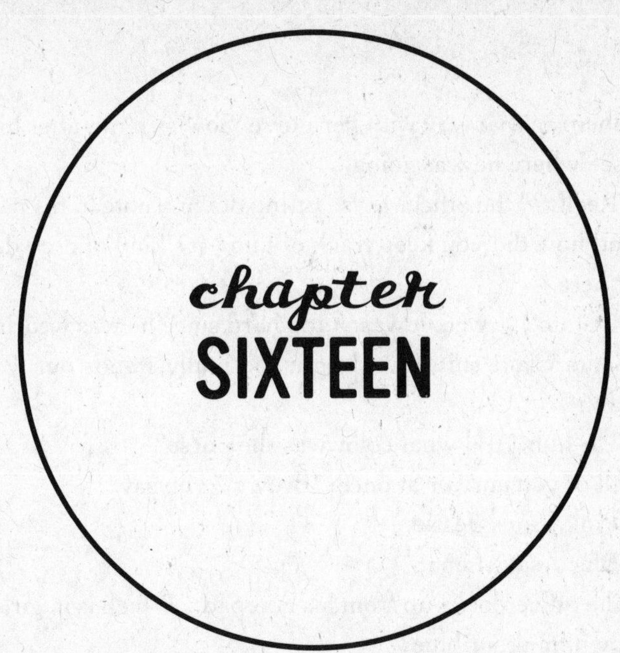

chapter SIXTEEN

You have a wild imagination. People like you tend to become writers, artists, and inventors, to name just a few of the possibilities. You tend to dream in color and in vivid detail about crazy things that have never happened to you in real life. That's because even while you're asleep, your creative mind is working overtime, which makes life more interesting. But be careful not to lose touch with reality altogether. There is a time and place for everything, and sometimes you need to deal with the real world as it is, and not as you imagine it to be.

"Well . . . ," you begin, casting nervous glances at Lena and Jessie, praying that they'll play along, "it's like this. We got here and were totally going to wait for you. But then we saw this woman get mugged and the robber ran that way with her purse. So we all ran after him to see where he was going."

"Really?" the officer says, jotting down a note in his pad. "And how did you keep track of him? It's kind of crowded out here."

"Oh, uh . . . well, it wasn't too hard since he was wearing a Santa Claus suit. That bright red really stands out, you know?"

"Uh-huh. And what color was the purse?"

All of you answer at once. "Brown," you say.

"Pink," says Jessie.

"Blue," says Lena.

The officer looks up from his notepad. "Which is it, girls? Brown, pink, or blue?"

"Um . . . all three," you reply. "Yeah, it was sort of like a peacock-colored purse with all different colors."

"Oookay," the officer says, casting a look at Amanda, who crosses her arms in front of her. "And how did this bad guy manage to get away? If there was a getaway car, we could trace it."

"No, no, there was no car," you say, urging your brain to think faster. "There would have been too much traffic, so he grabbed one of those horse and carriages, pulled the driver out, and galloped away." You point toward a path lined densely with trees, leading into Central Park.

The police officer heaves a heavy sigh and drops his arms. "So let me get this straight. A mugger in a Santa suit robbed a woman of her peacock-colored purse and then because three thirteen-year-old girls were chasing him, he stole a horse and carriage and took off into the park. Is that what you're telling me?"

You bite your lip and avoid eye contact. When you hear it all together like that, your story sounds ridiculous. But you have no choice but to commit at this point. "Uh . . . yes?"

"You do know that if this really happened, both the purse and the horse and carriage would have been reported stolen, and I can find out if there's been a report filed with one quick phone call to my precinct. Excuse me while I go confirm your story. It should only take a second. Oh, and just so you know, lying to a police officer is considered a crime. Good thing you three would never do a thing like that. Okay, be right back, ladies."

He turns away and starts ambling toward his squad car. Suddenly you are picturing yourself sitting in the backseat, begging Amanda to call your mom to get you out of jail.

"Wait!" you and your friends all cry, reaching toward the officer.

"Yeah?" He turns back nonchalantly, like he knew you wouldn't let him get all the way to his car. "Something you girls wanna tell me?"

You sigh heavily. "Okay, there was no mugger and no purse."

"And I'm guessing no Santa suit involved either, right?"

You shake your head miserably.

"Good. Why don't you try the truth this time?"

Jessie shrugs. "I saw somebody that I thought was a Jonas brother, so we ran after him. We didn't realize how far we'd run, but I guess it was pretty far, because by the time we got back, you were here."

"Is that it?" Amanda asks.

You each nod your head.

"Was it a Jonas brother at least?"

You all shake your heads and stare at the ground.

Amanda purses her lips and rubs her temples with her fingers. It's the same gesture your mom makes when you're working her last nerve and she's fighting the urge to sell you to a traveling circus. She turns to the policeman, who is watching this whole scene with a smirk of amusement. "I'm so sorry to have wasted your time, Officer. Thank you for all your help."

"No problem, miss," he says, adjusting his heavy belt. "And you girls, stay outta trouble, will ya?"

You nod and fold your hands in front of you the way you do at school when you're trying to look as innocent as humanly possible. For all you know, he could still lock you up just to teach you a lesson, and an orange jumpsuit would definitely clash with your complexion.

After the squad car speeds away, Amanda shakes her long brown hair out of her almost completely undone bun. Then she runs one hand through it and sighs deeply. But she doesn't say a word. Somebody's got to break the silence.

"So . . . what now?" you ask, scared to hear the answer. Do people still get tarred and feathered these days? You read about that in your history book and it sounds . . . unpleasant. Probably a college student wouldn't have tar handy, although the feathers would be easy enough. . . .

"I haven't decided yet," Amanda says at last. "On one hand, after the morning I've had, I'm not sure I can handle you three. Maybe I should just return you to your class trip and let your teachers deal with you. On the other, if I thought you were really sorry about all this, I might want to take you somewhere that would open your eyes to the fact that there are more important things than scoping celebrities. But I need to know: Can you see that what you did was wrong?"

That's the million-dollar question. Too bad you're not sure how to answer it. Seriously, was getting on a runaway train, stalking a celebrity look-alike, lying to a police officer, framing innocent Santa Claus–suit wearers, and nearly causing Amanda a heart attack that bad? Couldn't those things have happened to anyone?

Your New York City adventure ended up being a little more adventurous than you bargained for. Who knew that a day that started so innocently (walking single file into a museum to view ancient treasures) would

end with you almost being sent to the slammer (okay, maybe that's an exaggeration, but there was a police car involved). But still, were any of the day's events really your fault? Amanda seems to think so. If you think so too, now would be a good time to own up to it and see if Amanda will give you a second chance. If not, you'll just have to end your time with Lena's cousin and hope she sees it your way one day. So what'll it be?

QUIZ TIME!

Circle your answers and tally up the points at the end.

1. **You accused the boy who sits next to you in math class of cheating off you during a test, and he got in major trouble. But when they compared the two tests, most of his answers were totally different from yours. Turns out he wasn't cheating after all! What's your next move?**
   - **A.** You stick to your story. He did glare over at you a lot during the test; you didn't just imagine that. He probably changed some of his answers just to cover his tracks.
   - **B.** Reluctantly accept the proof of his innocence, but insist that you had your reasons for thinking he cheated.
   - **C.** Mumble an apology to him and to your teacher. Then try to put the embarrassing episode behind you.
   - **D.** Apologize like crazy to him, your teacher, and the whole class. You feel terrible for having accused him of something he obviously didn't do. Next time you'll keep your crazy theories to yourself.

2. **You and your BFF have had a huge falling-out. (No need to rehash the sordid details, but let's just say it involved a borrowed pair of suede shoes, a sandy beach, and high tide.) How do you get past it?**

   A. You wait until she apologizes. Even if you were wrong, you would still rather maintain the silent treatment forever than actually admit it. Who lends a person suede shoes anyway? Clearly she was in the wrong.

   B. Wait until one of your parents makes you apologize. You know your friend is mad, but you still wouldn't have given in if someone hadn't forced you to.

   C. You end up apologizing to each other. You tell her how sorry you are for ruining her shoes, and she apologizes for flying off the handle about it. (It's not like you did it on purpose.)

   D. You apologize first and offer to save up to get her a new pair. You knew you shouldn't have worn those shoes to the beach, but you did it anyway. And even though you don't think you deserved the amount of yelling she did, you hate it when there's tension between you and find that apologizing always breaks the ice.

3. **You are on your way out to meet some friends at the mall when your mom warns you that it is going to rain and will be terrible weather for the pretty yellow sundress you bought over the weekend. But all you see are blue skies for miles! You wear the dress anyway and of course, the minute you get a few steps away from your house, the skies open up and it starts pouring. What do you do?**

A. Keep going to the mall anyway and show up soaking wet and sick as a dog. Nobody (*cough cough*) is going to tell you (*aaa-CHOO!*) when you should wear your yellow sundress! (*sniffle sniffle*)

B. Sneak in your back door to snag your raincoat and galoshes. You don't want to show up at the mall looking like you've just been through a car wash, but you don't want to hear your mom say "I told you so" either.

C. Come back home and say that you were only kidding about wearing the sundress. Ha-ha. You were just testing your mom's parenting skills. Yeah, that's it. . . .

D. Return home to the open arms of your mom, who is waiting for you with a dry towel and a sympathetic look in her eye. "Fine, you were right," you admit. "Can I have a ride to the mall—after I change?" You're not too proud to recognize when you've been bested.

4 **It's a gorgeous day out and you'd much rather go to the park than go to school. You convince two of your friends to cut school with you and have a picnic instead. Naturally, you get busted. When faced with all of your parents, you:**

A. blame your friends for exerting their peer pressure on you. They turn to you with faces full of shock at your betrayal, but it's either you or them!

B. lie and claim you were heading back to school, but got sidetracked looking for your friend's lost contact lens. It's a stretch, but it's worth a shot.

C. try appealing to their sense of justice. Seriously, is it really fair to force you three to go to school on a day like today? No one could blame you for wanting to enjoy the great outdoors. (Note: This one won't fly either, but they've gotta admire your moxie.)

D. admit you were the ringleader and take your lumps. Your friends will get in trouble anyway for going along with you, but at least their parents will know that it wasn't their idea, so maybe they'll forgive you later.

5. **A friend of yours started hanging out with a guy a few weeks ago who you swore was bad news. Granted, this opinion was based solely on the fact that he wears a lot of black clothes and has an emo haircut (a la Peter Parker in *Spider-Man 3* when he turns bad). And yet, since then, he has proven to be supersweet and attentive, treating your friend very well. Do you eat your words?**

A. No way! He'll show his true colors eventually, and when he does, your friend will know that you were just looking out for her.

B. You admit he seems nicer than you thought. But you're still going to keep a wary eye on him, and you advise your friend to do the same.

C. Begrudgingly, you agree that he isn't the dangerous jerk you thought he was. That doesn't mean she has to gloat about it, though. Sheesh.

D. Totally. You can't believe it, but he has turned out to be pretty awesome and your friend seems happy. You apologize for doubting him. For once, you're glad you were wrong. (Not that you plan to make a habit of it or anything.)

Give yourself 1 point for every time you answered **A**, 2 points for every **B**, 3 points for every **C**, and 4 points for every **D**.

—If you scored between 5 and 12, go to page *172*.

—If you scored between 13 and 20, go to page *167*.

chapter SEVENTEEN

The truth is your friend. **You've got your feet firmly planted on the earth and your head is nowhere near the clouds. Your buds tend to come to you when they need a reality check, and nothing appeals to you more than cold hard facts. It's great that you're so grounded, but every now and then it's okay to let your brain play. After all, imagination is the spark that led to some of the world's greatest inventions—like 3-D movies, airplanes, and the Snuggie. (Well, maybe not so much the Snuggie, but you get the gist.)**

You always hear people say that they wish they could go back in time and do things differently. But if you had your way? You'd have the power to fast-forward through moments just like this one.

You and your two best friends are standing on the corner

of Fifty-ninth Street and Lexington, firmly in the grip of the long arm of the law. Amanda and the officer she flagged down to help find you—you know, back when you thought it was just a *great* idea to leave the corner where you were supposed to meet Lena's cousin, causing her to think you'd been kidnapped or worse—are waiting for an explanation.

You'd love to tell them something that would seem perfectly reasonable, but the fact is, you've got nothing but the truth. You can't imagine any story you could come up with that would be even remotely plausible, anyway.

"Well, it's like this . . . ," you say seriously. "We saw someone that we thought was Nick Jonas and he was moving really fast. And we thought it might be our only chance to meet him, so we kind of had to follow him and—"

"She keeps saying 'we,'" Jessie interrupts you, "but it was all my idea. I'm the one who thought we should chase him. They just followed along. Lena didn't want to go, but we sorta talked her into it."

"I could have said no," Lena offers. "You two aren't the boss of me."

"All right," Amanda says, holding her hand up to stop you. "I think I get the picture." She turns to the policeman, who is standing by with an amused smirk on his face. "I'm so sorry to have wasted your time, Officer. Thank you for all your help."

"No problem," he answers, waving away her thank-you. "Just doing my job. I'm glad this had a happy ending. It's like they said in the play by that Shakespeare guy that my daughter was just in. Oh man, what was it?" He snaps his fingers, trying to jog his memory.

"All's well that ends well?" Lena offers, her face lighting up at the mention of the Bard.

"Yeah, yeah, that's it," the officer says, pointing a stubby index finger at Lena. "All's well that ends well. Aw, you shoulda seen my daughter in that," he says, tapping Amanda's arm with one heavy hand and smiling from ear to ear. "She was really great. A real star, that one." Then he quickly clears his throat and gets serious again. "But ladies, do me a favor: Stay outta trouble while you're visiting my fair city, or next time things might not end so well, *capisce*?" He lowers his head but raises his bushy eyebrows.

You and your friends nod over and over again, probably looking like bobbleheads. "Yes, sir," you say, speaking for all three of you. He can consider you scared straight.

The officer nods, tips his hat to Amanda, and heads back to his squad car. "Good day, ladies. Stay safe out there."

He speeds away, the red and white lights on his roof spinning as he merges into traffic, and then he's gone—leaving you with a still very stressed-out Amanda.

"So . . . what now?" you ask, not sure you even want to know the answer.

Amanda shoves one hand into her coat pocket, tapping her chin with the other. "I haven't decided yet. What you guys did was not too bright, but I'm glad you told me the truth. And I understand that you want to see celebrities while you're here, but that's not the most important thing in the world. It's not even the coolest thing to do in New York."

You are all agreeing with Amanda, but something in Jessie's body language says that she's not completely convinced.

"You know what?" Amanda says, smiling as if she's just been struck by sudden inspiration. "I was going to take you to see Times Square or F.A.O. Schwarz, but now I think I have a better idea." She steps off the sidewalk and holds her arm straight up in the air. At first you think she's doing her Superman impression or something, which seems weird. But then you realize that she's hailing a cab. In seconds, a big yellow taxi with two rows of leather seats pulls up and you all pile in, Amanda snagging the seat next to the driver.

"Where to?" he asks Amanda.

She tells him an address, rubbing her hands together for warmth.

"Where are we going?" Lena asks nervously, watching the cab driver dart in and out of lanes as if he's playing some racing game on Wii.

"She said it was better than Times Square," answers Jessie. "So . . . maybe the Empire State Building? Or . . . oh! Maybe we're heading to the Village? That would be sweet!"

Amanda turns around. "Nope. Someplace even sweeter." She smiles mysteriously, and that's all she says as you zoom down the street.

You left the museum in hopes of seeing way more of New York than your class was going to see on the field trip. But so far, all you've seen are a crowded subway station and a faux Nick Jonas. And since you chose to ignore Amanda's directions to stay put in order to do a little celebrity stalking, she now thinks you need to get your priorities straight. You have no idea where she's planning to take you, but if it's sweeter than Times Square, it must be out of this world. Bring it on!

QUIZ TIME!

No quiz this time, sister. You're being held captive in a New York City cab and there's no getting out now. So just strap on your seat belt and hang on for the ride to page 167.

chapter EIGHTEEN

Your name might as well be SpongeBob, because you're just a touch self-absorbed. While it's true that everyone is the star of his or her own life, in *your* movie, you're the star, the supporting cast, the writer, the director, and the crew! It's great that you find your life so interesting and that you value your own experiences. But there's a whole world out there that is just begging you to sit up and take notice.

Times Square is even more amazing than you thought it would be. Everywhere you look are flashing neon signs, video billboards for all the hottest clothing lines and Broadway shows, and tons of restaurants and souvenir shops. As you walk down the busy sidewalk next to Amanda, you weave through groups of tourists from all over the world—some speaking German, some speaking Japanese, some speaking languages you don't even recognize! Every few feet you are handed a flyer for a comedy club or an electronics store. And in the middle of all this chaos is a pedestrian plaza where people are sitting outside, lounging at little plastic tables as if they were in a café in Paris during the summer instead of New York City in forty-degree weather.

"Wow, how cool is this?" you ask Lena, who has been awfully quiet since you left F.A.O. Schwarz. She must still be thinking about the cute duet you played with Amanda on the keyboard. That will definitely go down as one of the best moments of this trip for you.

"Uh-huh," she says now.

"Yeah," Jessie adds. "It's superfab. I just wish we had gotten here in time to see you-know-who at you-know-where."

When Amanda told you she was taking you to Times Square, Jessie immediately requested that you head straight to MTV Studios to see if you could catch a glimpse of Nick or, if you were really lucky, get his autograph. But when you arrived, the guard downstairs told you that Mr. Jonas had left five minutes before. Even worse, the guard wasn't sure where Nick's next promotional stop would be. Bummer. In a city this size, he could be anywhere! After that, Lena didn't want to hear any more about it, having listened to Jessie obsess over him all morning.

In your opinion, a celebrity sighting would have been cool, but you're just as happy getting to hang with Amanda, who has turned out to be cool and funny and who seems to think you're awesome too. You have been talking her ear off nonstop since the duet. (Someone had to pick up the slack, since Lena is being such an introvert and Jessie is busy mourning her missed opportunity.)

"Where are we going now?" you ask Amanda.

"Well, since I already took you to one famous toy store, I figured we should continue the theme. Everybody stick together!" You cross a noisy intersection and see the big Toys 'R' Us sign lit up in green, yellow, red, and purple. Leading out of the oversize revolving door is a line of people stretching down the block.

"You have to wait on line to get in?" Jessie asks, her eyes widening. "It's like getting into an exclusive party or something."

Amanda giggles a little and explains that there isn't usually a line, but around the holidays, shoppers descend on this store as if it's the last glass of water in the middle of a desert. "The line is to make sure no one gets trampled."

"Trampled?" Lena slows her walk. "Are we sure we want to go in there?"

"Definitely," Jessie insists, taking a place on line. "Check out what's inside!"

You take a peek through the thick glass windows, shielding the glare of the sun with your hands. "Is—is that—a Ferris wheel?" you stammer.

It is! Right smack in the middle of the store is a huge yellow Ferris wheel with little carriages built for two.

The line moves pretty quickly, and when you get downstairs to the Ferris wheel entrance, there's another line. But it's worth it. As soon as your crew gets to the front of the line, you jump into an M&M-themed car with Amanda, leaving Jessie and Lena to share the Cabbage Patch Kids car.

"This is sick! Do you come here every day?" you ask Amanda. "I would come every day if I lived here."

Amanda laughs out loud. "I don't think my professors would approve if I skipped class every day to ride a Ferris wheel."

"Oh, right. School." You rub your chin between your fingers. "I think I would just get a laptop and Skype with the professor from here."

"Note to self: Get a laptop and learn how to Skype," Amanda says, grinning.

"Lena could show you. Since she started her blog, she's picked up a ton of computer skills."

"She writes a blog?" Amanda asks, surprised. "I didn't know."

"Yeah," you go on, "and you should read it. A lot of it is about me. Maybe she'll turn it into a book one day and I'll be famous!"

Amanda chuckles again. You can tell you are totally cracking her up. Too bad you don't live in New York. If you did, you and Amanda would probably hang out all the time.

As you get to the top of the wheel, you take in a view of the whole store . . . and it rocks! You can see people strolling past on every floor, a lot of them staring at the Ferris wheel with wonder. And you can hear the roar of the mechanical T. rex on the lower floor in the *Jurassic Park* section. You pull out your camera and scoot closer to Amanda. "We've got to get a picture of us with all this behind us," you say. You hold out your arm as far as you can, aiming the camera at yourself. "Say cheese!"

"Cheeeese," Amanda repeats, holding up a peace sign behind your head to give you rabbit ears. You hope Jessie and Lena are having as much fun in their car as you are in yours.

When the ride finally comes to an end, you climb out, feeling jazzed. You also feel like your bladder is about to explode. Amanda walks the three of you through the section with all the baby supplies to the ladies' room. She says she'll be waiting right outside while you girls "powder your noses."

"Oh man, this is so much fun," you shout to Lena and Jessie from inside your stall. "I can't wait to see all the pictures. I got a really good one of Amanda and me on the Ferris wheel." You come out of your stall and walk over to the sink to wash your hands. Lena is already there, drying her own hands with a rough brown paper towel. "And I wasn't sure I'd have much in common with a college kid, but Amanda is so easy to talk to. Don't you think?"

Lena glares at you and you can see the muscles in her jaw

pulsing. "I wouldn't know," she says through clenched teeth. "I've barely gotten to say two words to her all day because somebody I know has been stuck to her like superglue!" With that, she storms out of the bathroom, leaving you in utter shock.

Jessie then swings open her stall door and inches out, wincing at what she just overheard.

"Uh . . . I'm confused. What's with her?" you ask, genuinely puzzled.

"You mean you really don't know?" Jessie asks while she washes up.

"Enlighten me."

"Well," Jessie says, drying her hands and then reaching up to tighten her ponytail, "we're only here for one day, which means Lena has only one day to see Amanda. And don't take this the wrong way, but you have been totally hogging her."

"Me? What about you! You've been talking to Amanda too."

"Yeah, but you've been way worse. I haven't said anything because I figured you'd get the hint eventually, but you just haven't noticed."

You are outraged! How could she accuse you of being so oblivious? "How do you figure I've been worse?"

"Let me count the ways," Jessie says, counting off on her fingers. "In F.A.O. Schwarz, Lena was going to play that duet with Amanda, but you jumped in front of her. Just walking around, you've been right next to Amanda the whole time and talking to her nonstop. And then we get here and you jump into the Ferris wheel car with Amanda without even asking Lena if she wanted that spot. And now you start bragging about how much fun *you're* having with Amanda and how *you two* took a picture together . . . I mean, what did you expect? Lena's pretty mild-mannered, but a girl can only take so much."

"But—but I was talking to Amanda about Lena on the Ferris wheel."

Jessie tilts her head sympathetically as if to say, *Aw, you poor clueless dope.* "Think about it this way." Jessie holds her hands out, palm side up, as if they are scales. "If I had the choice between someone talking to Nick Jonas about me"—she lowers her right hand—"or me getting to talk to him myself"—she lowers her left—"which one do you think I'd pick?"

Without even having to think about it, you tap her left hand, sinking the imaginary scale with the weight of your hand. "Eureka! I think she's got it," Jessie says in a game-show-host voice to a phantom audience.

"But I just think Amanda's awesome, that's all. I wish she were my cousin."

"Yeah, but she's not your cousin. She's Lena's."

You're floored. Have you really been that clueless all day? You thought Lena seemed extra quiet ever since you left the museum. Now that you think back on it, she didn't really seem all that thrilled when you and Jessie decided to tag along. And so far, Amanda was taking you all to do things that she thought you and Jessie would like. If it were just Lena and her cousin, they probably wouldn't even be in Times Square right now. They'd be off touring Amanda's college campus, maybe, talking about the future—and Lena would be on cloud nine.

You've been so wrapped up in your own good time that you didn't even realize you were ruining Lena's.

"I guess I'd better go apologize," you say. "I don't think she wants me to talk to her, though."

"Try singing your apology, then," Jessie jokes. "It always works on *Glee*!"

You come out of the bathroom fully prepared to face a scowling Lena. (Thankfully, Lena usually uses her powers for good, but she definitely knows how to kill you with a glare when she wants to.)

But what you see instead is Lena and Amanda sitting on a nearby window ledge, hugging and laughing. They are so deep in conversation that they don't even notice you and Jessie standing there until you clear your throat.

"Oh, hey, guys," Amanda says finally, sliding an arm around Lena's shoulders. "Lena and I have been talking and . . . Well, I was going to take two back to meet up with your class after this, since I haven't had enough quality time with my cuz here." She ruffles Lena's silky brown hair. "But how would you guys feel about coming with us to see where I work? I'm not sure you'll like it, but Lena really wants to go."

You shift your feet, not sure what Lena would want you to say. "Uh . . . I don't know. Lena, if you don't want me to go, it's cool."

You look at the shiny white-tiled floor. Lena stands up and crosses over to you, takes your hand, and pulls you off to the side. "Don't be such a lunkhead," she says. "I want you to come. And I'm sorry for biting your head off before. Amanda saw how upset I was when I came out of the bathroom and we talked about it. I guess I should have spoken up sooner."

"I'm sorry too," you say immediately. "I didn't know I was being so me, me, me."

Lena shrugs. "I just really missed Amanda and was a little jealous of all the time you two were spending together. But I get it. Like you said, she's awesome."

You look back at your Shakespeare-quoting, blog-writing, track-running, book-loving friend and smile. "It runs in the family."

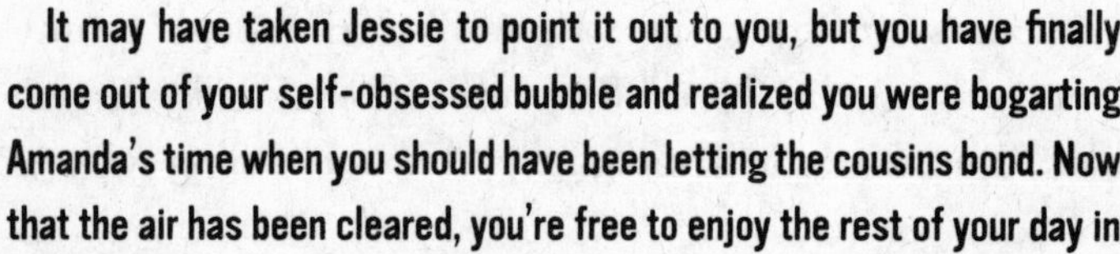

It may have taken Jessie to point it out to you, but you have finally come out of your self-obsessed bubble and realized you were bogarting Amanda's time when you should have been letting the cousins bond. Now that the air has been cleared, you're free to enjoy the rest of your day in

the city—only now you're going to do something Lena wants to do for a change. If whatever it is turns out to be half as cool as Lena, you'll have a blast.

QUIZ TIME!

No need for a quiz this time. Now that you and Lena are on the mend, you'll go wherever she leads. And right now, she's leading you to page 167.

chapter NINETEEN

Too bad you can't be cloned, because there should be more people like you. You don't have a self-absorbed bone in your body and are always in tune with what's going on with the world at large, your fam, your friends, even your pet hamster. And not only are you aware of things outside your own life, you actually care about them! That attitude is the stuff philanthropists and good friends are made of. But be careful not to put yourself on the back burner. It's okay to be just as interested in your own life as you are in everyone else's.

It's official: Lena is mad at you. She won't come out and say it, but you know the telltale signs: the pouty bottom lip; the crossed arms, as if she is literally trying to hold her anger inside; the one-word answers. Yep, you've been on the wrong side of Lena before and this stage is usually the calm before the storm. And you know why, too.

After you left F.A.O. Schwarz, you started going over the triumphant keyboard duet moment in your mind. When you watch the mental instant replay, you see Amanda ask if any of you know "Chopsticks," and you see Lena take a step forward with a gleam in her eye.

But then (and this is the part you wish you could leave on the cutting-room floor), you jumped in ahead of Lena and stole a moment with her cousin that should have been hers. D'oh! Oh well. You can't take it back now. What's done is done. But the day isn't over yet and maybe there's still time to make amends.

You've just come from the MTV Studios, where you struck out at meeting Nick Jonas. "Five minutes," Jessie keeps saying woefully. "I can't believe we missed him by five measly minutes."

"And I can't believe you've been saying that for half an hour," Lena complains. "Let it go already!"

Jessie lifts her eyebrows in surprise. "Soo-oo-oorry," she says, shooting you a *What's eating her?* look. If you could, you'd tell Jess that you and she are both guilty of horning in on Lena's reunion with her cousin, and then pushing Amanda to take you to see the stuff you and Jessie want to see. (Lena thinks Nick Jonas is okay, but she definitely wouldn't have chosen to spend any time trying to hunt him down.) And considering that Lena spent so much time supporting you and Jessie when you were dealing with the choir auditions, and has sat through numerous *Gossip Girl*-athons when she would much rather have been checking out a play or a new book, you both owe her big-time.

What you need to do is figure out a way to show Lena that you care about her feelings and aren't too dense to notice you've put her in a foul mood.

You tap Lena on her shoulder. "Hey. Is there anything you wanted to see? This is your day with your cousin, after all."

Lena seems surprised that you would even ask. She looks to Amanda and says, "I wouldn't mind seeing something that you haven't seen yet either, so we can see it for the first time together."

Amanda smiles at Lena's thoughtfulness. "Well, there is one place I've been wanting to go that I just haven't gotten around to yet, since I've been so busy with classes. It's kind of cheesy, and I'm embarrassed to say this, but . . . would you girls be up for seeing the Empire State Building?"

Lena breaks out in a huge smile. "Definitely!"

One short cab ride later and you're on Thirty-fourth Street. By the time you get to the observation deck of the Empire State Building, you're already dizzy! To get to the top, you have to go through a maze of hallways and stairs and ride at least two different elevators. It's crazy! And the elevators zoom up to the top so fast, your stomach rises into your throat around the time you hit floor 101. (You can't believe it when Amanda tells you that sometimes they have races for charity here and participants take the stairs from the first floor all the way to the top. Insane! You'd probably pass out by the time you got to the twenty-fifth floor.)

But now that you've reached the observation deck, you see that all the climbing was worth it. Even though the wind is so strong you feel like you would get blown away if the whole balcony weren't fenced in, the view is beautiful. "Lena, check it out!" you cry. "You can see the whole city from here! Hey, look, there's our class, and there's Jimmy," you joke, pretending to wave at an ant-size figure below. "Hi, Jimmy!"

Lena giggles happily, taking out her camera. "Don't forget Lizette and Charlie. I hope the blogging is going okay!"

"I'm sure you left the blog in capable hands. Now, how about a picture of the happy family reunion?" you suggest. You wave over Amanda, who had been checking out the scenery through one of the viewfinders on the deck, and motion the two of them into a corner, where clusters of steel skyscrapers and puffy clouds that look like snowballs form the perfect backdrop. Amanda pulls Lena in front of her and hugs her from behind, pressing her cheek against Lena's. "Say N-Y-C!" you chirp.

"N-Y-C!" they echo loudly. *Flash.*

As you head back down the first bank of elevators, Amanda digging around in her bag for her phone so that she can call your teacher and let her know you're on your way, Lena reaches over and squeezes your hand. You recognize that telltale sign too. It means *I forgive you* and *thanks*.

It's been a crazy day, but right now life couldn't get any sweeter.

THE END

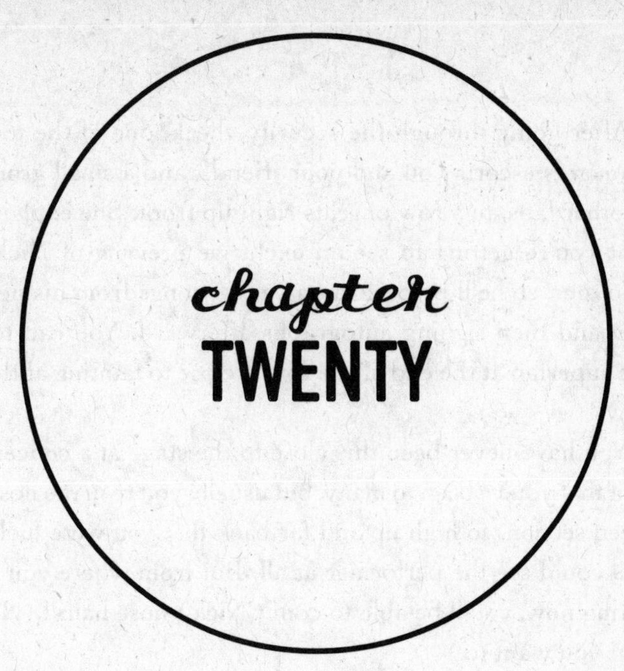

Even though this is supposed to be one of the smaller venues in Madison Square Garden, the theater where Nick Jonas will be performing for thousands of screaming fans next week is enormous, and it looks even bigger right now since it's practically empty.

After going through the security check, one of the tour managers escorts you and your friends, and a small group of other fans, to a row of seats right up front. She explains that you're getting to see an exclusive preview of Nick's solo tour, so he'll be performing a few songs from his new CD and then signing autographs afterward. You can tell the superfan at the end of the row is close to fainting at this news.

You have never been this close to the stage at a concert. Not that you've been to many, but usually you're in the nose-bleed section, so high up and far back that you were lucky you could see the performer at all. But from where you're sitting now, you'll be able to count Nick's nose hairs! (Not that you want to.)

"This can't really be happening, can it?" you ask your friends. "I'm probably daydreaming and this one is really, reeeally vivid."

"Bite your tongue!" Jessie shouts next to you. "This is *so* happening. And if it isn't and you've just pulled us into your daydream somehow, then please keep dreaming for *at least* the next hour!"

Lena giggles on the other side of you. "I don't know about you, but in my daydreams I never get sweated on by a roadie moving equipment around."

You all look up at the stage, where a lanky guy around Amanda's age dressed in a black T-shirt and black pants is shoving a heavy amp across the floor. Every few steps, he stops, stands up, and shakes his head like a dog, sending beads of sweat flying everywhere.

"Ew!" Jessie recoils, totally repulsed.

Amanda leans over so that she can talk to all three of you. "You do know that Nick will probably be sweating too, right? Those are the hazards of sitting in the first row."

"That's different!" Jessie argues. "I bet even his sweat is talented. Besides, even if it isn't, I could catch it in a napkin, put it up on eBay, and make a fortune!"

You all laugh at the thought of some rabid fans using up their college savings to bid on a sweaty napkin. It wouldn't be unheard of!

It seems like forever goes by while the crew does multiple mike checks, and whoever is controlling the lighting runs through the sequence once, twice, four times. First blackness, then a single white spotlight, then the stage erupts into color from above and below.

You're all getting antsy now. "Come on, where is he?" Jessie whines, hopping up and down in her seat.

And as if she had summoned him, Nick Jonas walks onto the stage in a simple white T-shirt and jeans, his bushy black hair looking slightly tousled and a guitar strapped to his back. He walks toward the single microphone stand and does a quick "One two, one two" into it. Then he glances down and smiles as if he has just noticed the group of you there. "Oh, hey!" he says sweetly. "Glad you guys could make it. Let me know how this sounds, all right?"

OMG! Nick Jonas is, like, asking for your opinion. That was practically a *conversation* you had!

He swings the guitar around to the front and gives someone offstage a cue, then the houselights dim while he plays the opening chords of a ballad he wrote for this album.

It. Is. AWESOME!

The three or four songs he plays go by so quickly, the last one leaving all of you on your feet, jamming along with him.

When he finishes, you all go crazy, applauding so hard and for so long that your hands hurt. There are only about twenty fans there, but you make such a ruckus, it sounds like there are two hundred.

Afterward, Nick climbs down from the stage, takes a seat behind a small table to the right, and has his manager hand him a black Sharpie and a stack of CDs. The assistant has you line up in front of the table and, one by one, Nick autographs the CD (a sample set he made exclusively for the winners of these passes—not even available on iTunes yet!), takes a picture with the fan, and shakes his or her hand. Amanda sits this part out, preferring to act as your paparazzi, taking pictures of all three of you as you wait in line and then as you meet Nick Jonas himself.

"Oh my God, you're so fabtastic," Jessie gushes when she gets to the front of the line. "I'm your biggest fan. Thank you, thank you, thank you!"

"Breathe, Jess," you whisper from behind her. "Don't forget to breathe!"

Jessie takes a deep breath and tries to rein herself in, but squeals anyway when she shakes his hand. (Jessie wouldn't be Jessie without the squeal.)

"Sorry about that," you tell Nick, feeling very mature when it's your turn. "My friend is just excited."

Nick shrugs. "That's all right. I love it that my fans get so pumped. They love music just as much as I do. I wish my brothers had been here to see this, though. Everything seems more fun when we're together, you know?" He looks up at you with sincere brown eyes.

You glance over at your two best friends, and your brand-new friend Amanda, as they chatter happily a few feet away.

"Yep. I know exactly what you mean," you answer.

After that, you and Nick Jonas talked for three hours, and he invited you and your friends onto his tour bus to meet his family and eventually go on tour with them and Demi Lovato.

Psych!

You wish. That didn't happen, but you did have a signed CD to show off to your friends when you got back on the bus heading for home. And Jimmy, who had been a little upset that you ditched the school trip instead of staying to hang with him, forgave you once you told him about the rocky start to your adventure and how scared you were.

"Sounds intense," Jimmy says, his deep green eyes looking even darker as you pass into the shadow of the Lincoln Tunnel. "Good thing you had Jessie and Lena with you. But I wish . . ." He bows his head shyly. "I wish *I* could have been there with you."

You smile. Just when you think your ice cream sundae of a day can't get any sweeter, Jimmy comes along and puts a cherry on top.

THE END

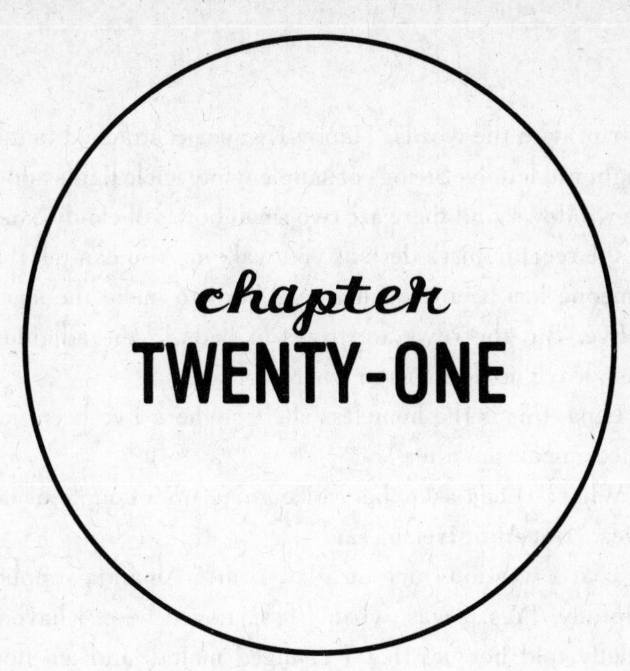

chapter TWENTY-ONE

You were totally expecting to walk into a fancy law firm, weren't you? Well, this place is no law firm. There's a huge lobby with a TV in one corner and a few rows of simple chairs in front of it, and a coffee table with a miniature Christmas tree, a menorah, and a small basket of fruit with the words "Happy Kwanzaa" attached to it in bright red letters. Strings of simple white icicle lights adorn the windows, and there are two small bowls of candy canes on the receptionist's desk as you walk in. You can tell that someone has been working very hard to make the space festive. But the rows and rows of beds in the adjoining room leave no doubt as to where you are.

"Lena, this is the homeless shelter where I've been volunteering all semester."

"What?" Lena asks, her voice going up a couple of octaves. "But Aunt Helena said—"

"That I was interning at a law firm?" Amanda supplies helpfully. "Yes, I was, when I first moved here. I haven't exactly told her yet that I changed majors and am now studying social work."

"Really? But why didn't you tell me? I'm the last to know everything!"

"Actually, I haven't told anyone yet," Amanda corrects her gently. "You're the first. I'm just not sure how Mom and Dad are going to react, since I know they wanted me to follow in their footsteps. But after I moved here I started to see that my heart wasn't in corporate law. I wanted to help people. And there are a lot of people in this city who could use my help."

"Amanda, sweetie!" a smiling woman with frizzy black hair calls from across the room. "You're back . . . and I see you've brought friends."

"Yes, hi, Linda," Amanda answers, giving the woman a

quick hug. "This is my cousin and her two friends from school." You all shake hands and tell Linda your names. "I know they're a little young," Amanda starts apologetically, "but do you think they could help out here for a little while? Can you put them to work?"

You start to crack a joke about child labor laws, but all the volunteers around you seem to be knocking themselves out and you don't want to seem like a brat.

"Of course!" Linda says, clapping her hands together. "There are always a million and one things to do around here. Why don't we start with the coats?"

Amanda tells you that every winter around this time, the city has a coat drive. Anybody can donate gently used coats so that someone who doesn't have a coat can be warm. You wouldn't have believed it if you hadn't seen it with your own two eyes, but the donation room is overflowing with coats and jackets of every color and size. Linda explains that your job will be to sort the coats by size, and make a separate pile for children's sizes. The shelter will be giving them away after dinner today.

The very fact that there are kids out there who don't have coats to get through the harsh New York winters makes you realize how lucky you and your friends are. As you, Jessie, and Lena work, you think you'll never complain about your bulky blue parka or funny-looking green pom-pom hat again.

After you finish with the coats, Amanda calls you over to take part in the dinner service. You each get to don plastic gloves, aprons, and hair nets, and as the guests file past you with a cardboard tray, you put a scoop of vegetables on their plate, Lena adds a scoop of pasta, Jessie adds a soft dinner roll, and Amanda ladles out a small cup of tomato soup. "Here you go, George," she says kindly to an older man with a tangled gray beard and wrinkled eyelids.

George smiles gratefully at her and takes a seat at the long table that looks a little like the cafeteria benches in your school.

"Are all these people going to live here forever?" Lena whispers to Amanda.

"No—the staff work very hard to find everyone permanent homes, but it's easier said than done," Amanda explains. "So until then, we just make sure they have a hot meal and a warm place to be, at least for a little while."

If you didn't see how awesome Amanda was before, you definitely see it now. And you can see it on the face of each person coming through the line. Amanda is really helping them and trying to make a difference. You feel kind of silly that this morning your biggest dream was to shop in a chic New York boutique and hobnob with the rich and famous. You're starting to see that there are more important things. Like right now? You kind of think making George laugh would rank right up there with getting to ride in Diddy's private jet.

After everyone is served, Linda comes to the front of the room and announces that she has a special treat for everyone. "The carolers from the East Side Community

Center would like to sing a few songs for you." She hands out simple programs with the list of songs on the menu. You know every one of them by heart.

Your BFFs and you exchange excited looks.

It wasn't too long ago that you thought you might be singing in Carnegie Hall with your school. But now that you've seen the work they do in the shelter, you feel like singing here would feel even better.

You peel off your gloves and approach the choir director, in his slightly worn gray sweater and corduroy pants, as he pulls out a small silver pitch pipe to help everyone find the right note.

"Would you mind if my friends and I joined you?" you plead.

"Of course you can!" he says, rearing back in surprise. "The more, the merrier."

The other choir members help all of you find a position, and after you sing the starting note, the group launches into a happy rendition of "Let It Snow! Let It Snow! Let It Snow!"

You can see Amanda looking on with pride in her eyes in her seat next to George. You can't wait to get back to your class and tell the other kids about your New York City singing debut. Carnegie Hall would have been nice, but this is way, way sweeter.

THE END

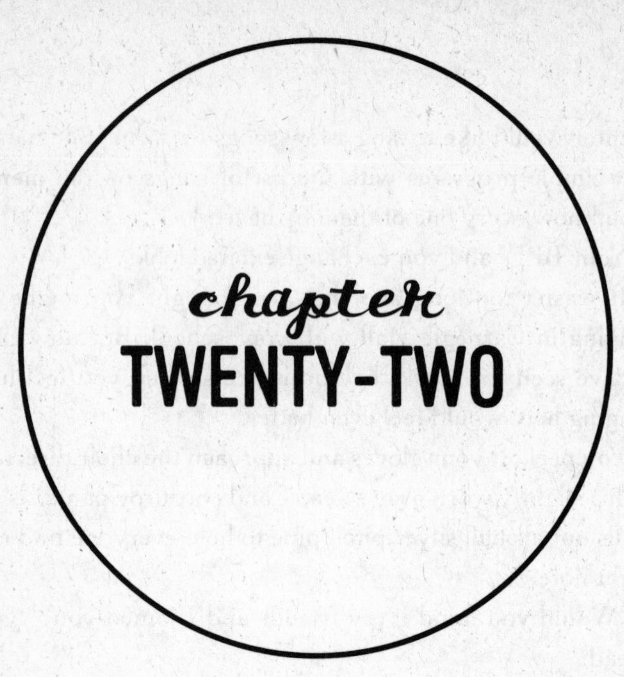

chapter TWENTY-TWO

You have mixed feelings walking into Radio City Music Hall with your class. Nothing has gone quite right today and you aren't sure what to expect. Sure, "Spectacular" is right in the title of the show, but so far your day has been anything but. And you're coming to the part you've been dreading most all day: sitting next to Mona. Even though you and Mona seem to have called a temporary truce, she can be unpredictable. You just never know with her. (You make a mental note to check for gum on your theater chair before you sit down.)

Meanwhile, you've texted Jimmy a couple of times during the day but never got a response. So you're guessing he's still mad at you too. The show would have to be extra-super-duper-spectacular to make you forget that.

"All right, kids!" Ms. Darbeau shouts over the din as you enter the plush lobby. "I expect all of you to be on your absolute best behavior in the theater. I mean it. If I see one spitball fly or if I hear one Jay-Z ringtone go off . . . you will be back on the bus for home in a heartbeat, got it?" She raises one eyebrow and eyeballs the lot of you.

"Yes, Ms. Darbeau," you all say in unison.

"Good." She nods curtly, and her stern face abruptly yields to one of sweetness and light. "Let's file in and enjoy the show! The ushers will lead you to your seats."

As you follow the usher down the red-carpeted aisle of the mezzanine section, listening to the orchestra tune up from some invisible location beneath the stage, the knot in your stomach pulls tighter. The last thing you wanted to deal with today was Mona. But now you're going to be stuck with her for the next hour and a half.

The usher leads you down to your row and you find your seat six chairs in. Seats fill in all around you, but the one to your left, Mona's seat, stays empty. For a moment you think maybe her model-agent mom picked her up to take her on a job or something and she won't be coming after all. Or maybe Mona is simply messing with your head, making you suffer through the anticipation of her arrival.

But just before the lights begin to dim, you see someone with shaggy brown hair and a dark gray coat sneak into your row and make his way to the empty chair. Jimmy Morehouse, your favorite artist.

"Wha . . . ?" you whisper, confused. "Mona, is that you? I had no idea you could do such a great Jimmy impression. You should take that show on the road!"

Jimmy smiles with one corner of his mouth. "Funny. Look, I'm as confused as you are. Mona found me in the lobby and told me to switch tickets with her. She said I could thank her later."

You are suddenly so grateful for the dark lights and the loud overture that has started booming from the front of the room. Otherwise Jimmy might see you turning eight shades of red and he might hear your heart booming like a drum.

"And . . . are you glad you did it, or are you plotting your sweet revenge against Mona right now?"

Jimmy smiles his half smile again, tucks a stray lock of brown hair behind his ear, and taps your knee with his. "I'm glad."

You're not sure what got into Mona, but you're glad too.

Soon the Rockettes storm the stage in their red and white outfits, kicking their legs in perfect unison across the floor while enormous Christmas ornaments descend from the ceiling. Each number they perform is bigger and better and more dazzling than the last.

But the truth? You would have been just as happy if you'd been watching a donkey pull a broken wagon across an empty stage, or if your principal got up there and read your school's conduct manual from cover to cover. You wouldn't even mind if Mark got up there and sang every Green Day song he knows for two hours straight. The only thing you needed to end this crazy day on a sweet note is sitting right next to you.

THE END

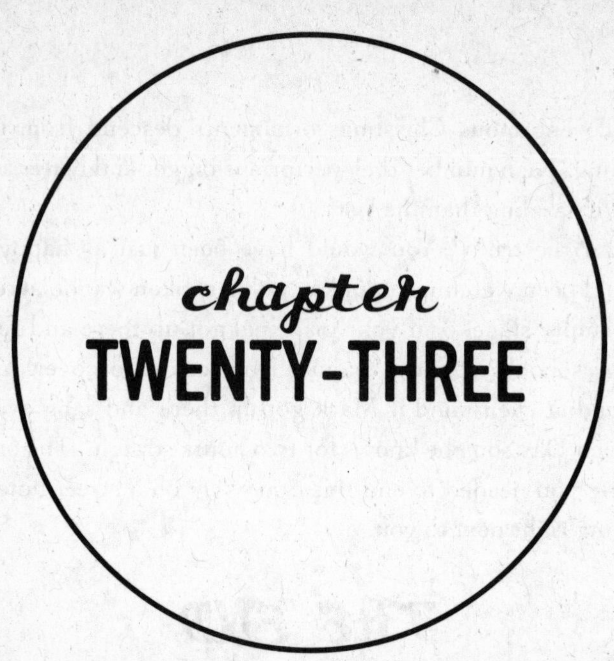

chapter TWENTY-THREE

You're a giver. **Generous to a fault, you are one of those people who would literally give someone the shirt off your back if they needed it, without a second thought. And you understand that giving your time and attention is even more important than giving things. Just be on the lookout for people who like to take advantage of kind souls like you. Give till it hurts, but not till you're unconscious!**

Was that you actually refusing to help Jimmy? That didn't even seem like you. True, you turned him down for what felt like a good reason (if Jessie were here, she would say the chance to meet Nick Jonas and score backstage passes was a very, *very* good reason), but still . . .

Even though he was asking you to help Mona, who seems to have made it her mission to drain all the joy out of your life, you know in your gut that lending a hand would have been the kinder thing to do. Mona might not deserve your help, but that doesn't mean you shouldn't give it to her anyway.

The worst part is that Jimmy was a witness to your temporary lapse in judgment. No use waiting. You need to get back there and check on Mona.

You glide off the ice and scan through the crowds of kids from your school until you spot Mona sitting on a bench between Jimmy and a staff member, who has brought over a chair so that Mona can elevate her ankle. If you had to guess, you'd say she's milking this a little bit, but when the staff member takes off her skate and pulls out an ice pack, Mona winces and you see that her ankle does look kind of swollen. And either your eyes are playing tricks on you, or Mona is shedding real tears—from pain or from embarrassment, you aren't sure. Great. Now you feel even worse for the way you acted earlier. If you had any doubts about what you are about to do, the pitiful sight of Mona dabbing at her eyes and scanning the room for Paul erases them.

You're walking purposefully toward Mona when Lizette blocks your path. "Hey, *chica,* where have you been? I've been looking for you. I need to interview you for the blog. Lena will kill me if I don't nail down some student perspectives on our trip so far." She pulls out a small notebook, filled with notes for Charlie to type in later.

"Sorry, Lizette. I can't right now. There's something I have to take care of first." Lena's nose for reporting must have rubbed off on Lizette, because she follows you over to Mona's bench, staying a few feet away with her pencil poised over the notebook.

"Hi, Mona," you say, pretending not to notice the fact that Jimmy is studiously ignoring you. "Are you all right? How's the ankle?"

"How does it look?" Mona snaps. "I think I may have sprained it, not that you care."

You knew that was coming. But you don't let Mona's acid tongue derail you. "I'm sorry I didn't help," you tell Mona honestly. "But I think I might have something that'll make you feel better."

"A new leg?" Mona asks.

"Better." You hand her the envelope with the four backstage passes inside.

She pulls them out and stares up at you. "Are these for real?"

"Yes. A publicist gave them to me on the ice-skating rink. Nick Jonas is going to be here in a minute and he's going to call for the girl who has those passes to join him in front of the news cameras."

"And you're giving them to me?" she asks.

"Yeah!" Lizette says now, unable to maintain the journalistic distance Lena always insists is rule number one. "You're giving them to *her*?"

"Yes," you say simply. Right now, you know Mona would

not want to hear that you're taking pity on her and that you think she needs them more than you do. So you come up with something she'll accept. "I know that since you're a model and all, you're comfortable in front of cameras, whereas I would be a deer in the headlights. You would really be the better choice."

"Can't argue with you there," Mona replies haughtily, smoothing down her luscious black hair and batting her baby blue eyes. She has her Mona mojo back just in time too, since Paul comes sauntering over right then.

"Hey, Mona, I saw you take a spill out there. Are you okay?"

"I'm fine now," Mona answers, full of bravado again. "But I might need your help in a second."

"Yeah? What for?"

Before she has a chance to answer, you all hear an announcement come over the loudspeaker. "Ladies and gentlemen, please clear the ice for our special surprise guest . . . Nick Jonas!"

There are gasps of shock all over the rink and a pack of security guards materializes, seemingly out of nowhere, to hold back the suddenly screaming fans. You note with amusement that even Holly Happy-Go-Lucky and Mary Sunshine, the two girls in school you would vote most likely to play Wednesday in *The Addams Family,* are among the horde of kids struggling to get past the guards.

Nick Jonas steps up to the microphone at the far end of the rink, where they have set up a simple platform covered in green felt. "Hello, New York!" More screams. "Can I please have the girl with the backstage passes to my concert up here for a minute? These nice photographers would like to take our picture!" Whereas before you saw only one TV camera, the news seems to have spread like wildfire: TMZ, FOX News, MTV . . . *Amy Choi must be in heaven right now,* you think, seeing so many of her gossip-spreading idols in one place.

"That's our cue," Mona says to Paul, reaching for his hand. He pulls her up onto her good leg, lets her throw an arm around his shoulder, and leads her through the wall of guards to the platform.

The woman who gave you the passes blinks with confusion when Mona comes into view. But you guess she figures it's better not to cause a scene with all the cameras watching. Besides, Mona may be a nightmare, but she's also a knockout. She looks pretty great next to Nick as the paparazzi go crazy snapping pictures of the two of them.

Lizette just stares at you with her jaw unhinged. "Have you lost your mind—you gave up Jonas tickets! *Tú eres loca!*"

"I'm not crazy," you assure your friend. "It was just . . . the right thing to do."

"Oh yeah? Tell that to Jessie when you see her. She's going to say it was the dumb thing to do."

Jimmy, who had been silent all this time, stands up and looks toward the news crews, seemingly taking note of how happy Mona looks up there. "I think it was kind of awesome," he says.

"Thanks, Jimmy," you say, hoping for a little eye contact. But no dice. Instead he walks away, leaving you to stare sadly after him.

Wow, that was a pretty big sacrifice you just made. Backstage passes to a concert is a huge score in anyone's book, and not only did you give them up, you gave them to your nemesis, a girl you spent half the day mentally sparring with. You're only human and you may not always take the highest moral ground where she's concerned, but when push came to shove (or in this case, when Mona's behind hit the ice), you came through in a big way as only you could. Lizette thinks you need professional help and Jessie will surely think you've gone mad, but at least you feel better. And obviously, so does Mona. You did a good thing, letting her have the spotlight she seems to need, but you can tell that Jimmy is still a little hurt about the way you treated him. You can't blame him. You just hope he can completely forgive you before you head home.

QUIZ TIME!

There's only one place to go from here. Head to page 172 to see if your last bite of the big apple is sweet—or if it has a big ol' worm in it.

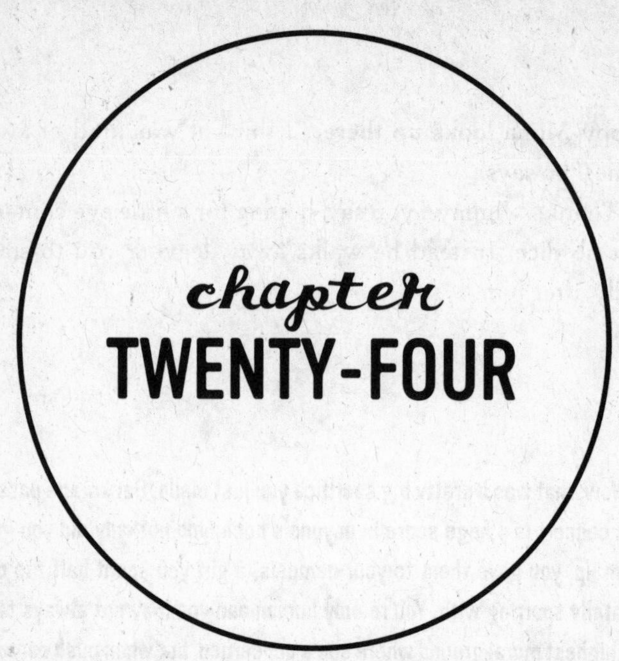

chapter TWENTY-FOUR

It may not be politically correct to admit this, but when you have to choose between giving and receiving, you pick receiving every time. Whether it's birthday presents or just loads of attention, you love it all, and it doesn't usually occur to you to reciprocate. The truth is, everybody likes to be the receiver of good things sometimes. They'd be lying if they said they didn't. (Why do you think celebs go to so many events? Swag!) But what you don't seem to be familiar with is how good it can feel to give. The people who receive houses on *Extreme Makeover: Home Edition* are thrilled to get a new home, but it's the hundreds of volunteers who build them that home who end up shedding tears of joy.

Normally you would jump at the chance to go just about anywhere with Jimmy. The tip of Antarctica during a hailstorm? Sure! Could be fun. Swimming in shark-infested waters in the middle of the ocean? Why not? At least one of the sharks in *Finding Nemo* was nice. But leave the ice-skating rink to help Mona, thus passing up a photo op with a Jonas brother? Puh-lease! You're not *that* into Jimmy.

You do feel kind of bad, though, as you watch him amble his way over to Mona and help her to her feet. He can barely maneuver himself on skates, so you know that helping a now-limping Mona must be a struggle. And you can't deny the sharp stab of jealousy that sticks in your gut as you watch Jimmy wrap an arm around Mona's waist. (He was awfully quick to run to her aid. Could he maybe be interested in her? Nah, that's crazy talk . . . right?)

But if Jessie were here, she'd back you up. Part of the reason you were so excited to come to New York in the first place is that you heard things like this—random celebrity sightings and unexpected winnings—happened all the time. And now it's happened to you! So you're not budging until you get your five minutes of fame while standing next to (IYHO) the cutest of the Jonas Brothers.

Still, that disappointed look in Jimmy's eyes stays in your mind like a bad movie. Could it be that you were wrong? Maybe you ought to go catch up with him and—

Before you even get to finish that thought, you hear an

announcement come over the loudspeaker. "Ladies and gentlemen, please clear the ice for our special surprise guest . . . Nick Jonas!"

There are gasps of shock all over the rink and a pack of security guards materializes, seemingly out of nowhere, to hold back the suddenly screaming fans. One of the guards guides you back toward one of the rink exits with everyone else. You note with amusement that even Holly Happy-Go-Lucky and Mary Sunshine are among the horde of kids struggling to get past the guards.

Nick Jonas steps up to the microphone at the far end of the rink, where they have set up a simple platform covered in green felt. "Hello, New York!" More screams. "Can I please have the girl with backstage passes to my concert up here for a minute? These nice photographers would like to take our picture!" Whereas before you saw only one TV camera, the news seems to have spread like wildfire: TMZ, FOX News, MTV . . . *Amy Choi must be in heaven right now,* you think, seeing so many of her gossip-spreading idols in one place. *Just wait until she gets a load of this!*

You tap the shoulder of a large guard with a Bluetooth hanging over his ear. "Excuse me," you say politely. "He's talking about me."

The guard, extending his arms to hold back the tide, looks at you over his shoulder and smirks. "Yeah, sure, you and every other girl in here," he says, dismissing you and turning back around again.

"Weak," Holly says to you.

"Yeah," Mary adds. "If you're going to lie, at least try to be convincing."

The nerve of them, thinking that you're lying! You'll show them convincing. You tap the guard's shoulder again.

He turns around with an exaggerated sigh, clearly ready to shoot you down once more. But this time you hold up the envelope you were handed earlier, waving it back and forth like a fan.

"Oh," the guard says, looking from the envelope to you, a touch of color flooding his face. "Come with me."

You follow him onto the ice, turning quickly to stick your tongue out at Holly and Mary. Ha!

The rest is a blur of camera flashes and excitement. It doesn't last long since Nick Jonas has other stops on his whirlwind publicity tour, but you're standing next to him (flashing your coveted backstage passes, of course) long enough to see that he looks even better in person than he does in the magazines. The rest of your classmates look sick with envy. (Eat your heart out, Mary!) And Jimmy looks . . . Well, Jimmy is nowhere to be found. It seems he is working hard to ignore you—a fact that becomes even more obvious as you file into your seats at Radio City Music Hall about a half hour later.

It's bad enough that you don't have either Lena or Jessie here with you to celebrate with (you texted them, but they must be having too much fun with Amanda to text back), but now Jimmy won't even look at you. You spot him sitting a few rows behind you, between Charlie and Kevin

Minks. As you listen to the orchestra tune up from somewhere below the stage, you turn in your seat and wave frantically, trying to get his attention. Charlie waves back and smiles, but Jimmy is pretending to be engrossed in his program. When you finally give up, you see the one person you least want to see right now: Mona Winston. She is hobbling toward you with brown ACE bandages wrapped around one ankle. Everyone in the aisle is heaping sympathy on her, offering to help carry her bag until she gets to her seat, or asking if she wants to sit closer to the aisle so that she won't have to hop so far.

"No, no, that's all right," she says with a syrupy sweet smile. "I'll get by somehow. Besides, I love my assigned seat." She locks eyes with you and the angelic innocent act drops for one quick instant, and you see the ruthless Mona you wish you didn't know so well.

As she settles into her seat, she turns to you and says, "Well, congratulations on those Jonas tickets. That's great. Of course, I would have been on the sidelines cheering for you, but as you can see"—she indicates her wrapped leg—"I was injured. I understand some people refused to help. Can you believe anyone could be so insensitive? Jimmy was telling me that girls who value things over people really bug him. Thank goodness Jimmy was there with me. He has been so sweet, refusing to leave my side for a moment! He even held the ice pack in place for me until they bandaged me up. He said he'd help me onto the bus on the way home. I told him that wasn't necessary, but he wouldn't take no for an answer. It's so nice to know that he cares about me so much." Mona sighs contentedly, stroking her thick black hair between her porcelain fingers.

There are a million responses you have on the tip of your tongue—most of them not so nice—but before you have a chance to let any of them fly, the houselights begin to dim while the stage lights come to life. Soon you are awash in a sea of brightly colored giant ornaments, fake snow, and what seems like an endless line of Rockettes, kicking in perfect unison and smiling as if not a thing in the world could be wrong.

If only you felt the same way.

"Okay, tell me again," Jessie urges you, after you and your BFFs have been reunited on the bus heading home. Once you told them what happened, Lena didn't want to be separated by a bus seat. So the three of you are squished into one row. "Only this time, speak very, very slowly."

"Jessie!" Lena whispers, trying not to wake your other classmates, most of whom are sleeping. (Mark Bukowski is all the way in the last row, but you can hear him snoring up a storm.) "She has already gone over this story three times! She told you: She was on the ice, she was chosen to win backstage passes, and then she met Nick Jonas. End of story."

"End of story? *End of story?*" Jessie says, grabbing her ponytail with both hands. "But I just can't believe it! And she didn't tell us what Nick was wearing, what he smelled like . . . Were his brothers there? Did he touch your hand at any point? If so, which one? And now we all get to go to the concert? Why aren't you more excited about this? Ugh, I could kick myself for not staying now!" She looks quickly over at Lena and smiles apologetically. "Not that I didn't have a superfab time with you and Amanda."

"Noted," Lena says with an eye roll. "But have you not noticed how sad and pathetic our friend here looks?" Lena reaches out and pinches your cheeks and feels your forehead with the back of her hand. "I don't think she's sick, so something must be wrong."

Jessie takes another long look at your hangdog expression and tilts her head curiously. "Now that you mention it . . . What happened?" Her eyes suddenly turn steely—well, as steely as Jessie's eyes ever get. "Does this have anything to do with M-O-N-A?" she whispers. "Was she up to her old tricks while we were gone?"

You shrug. "Not exactly." You fill them in on the ugly parts you left out of your story the first time around—your initial plot to steal Paul's attention away from Mona, your refusal to help Mona off the ice after she fell, and Jimmy giving you the cold shoulder ever since.

Jessie sits back with a huff once you're done and crosses her arms angrily. "Oh, and I'm sure she was just loving it, that little ferret. And then rubbing it in at Radio City . . . the nerve of her! I have a good mind to go stick the lollipops we bought at Toys 'R' Us right in her precious hair!"

"No, no," you say immediately, shooting her a grateful

glance. "Thanks for the thought, but I'm not sure candy warfare is called for here. The truth is, even though Mona is a little ferret, she was also right. I should have helped her off the ice, and I think it really disappointed Jimmy that I wouldn't. And now I think he might like her again—"

"Again?" Lena interrupts. "According to my notes"—she quickly takes out her BlackBerry and scrolls through her blog's archives—"the date the two of them had planned for Shawna's party was one of convenience, not because he actually liked her. See here?" She nudges the screen in your direction.

"I know, I know," you mumble, without even looking at the screen. "But what if that wasn't the whole reason? What if he did think she wasn't so bad back then? And what if now that he's seen how amazing she is on skates, and he's spent all this time with her, he thinks she's kind of cool? My crummy behavior sure didn't help things."

"Aw, I'm sure you weren't that bad. And besides, you were acting that way for a really good reason: Nick Jonas! Helloooo? Why don't you just give Jimmy the fourth pass? I'm sure all will be forgiven once we're at the concert together."

You would so love to believe that, but you know it just isn't that simple. In fact, you know exactly what you have to do, but Jessie and Lena aren't going to like it, not one bit.

"Guys, I'm really sorry, but I won't be going to the concert with you."

"What?" Jessie shrieks, causing a still half-asleep Mark

to snort himself awake in the back and shout out, "That is not the real Santa Claus!" before dozing off again.

"What do you mean you aren't going?" Jessie asks with a horrified look on her freckled face.

"I mean," you answer, scooting past her to stand up in the aisle and draw your two passes out of your back pocket, "I'm giving mine to someone who deserves them."

Before Jessie or Lena have a chance to stop you, you make your way toward the front of the bus where Jimmy and Charlie are sitting, sharing an iPod and eating M&M's. "Um. Hey, Jimmy," you start nervously, not sure if he'll just shoo you away right here. He looks up suddenly and an instant smile flashes on his face, before his memory of the day sets in and his expression goes back to neutral.

"Hey."

"Uh, would you mind if I talked to you for a second?"

He looks at you, seeming to weigh his options, then shrugs and says, "Sure." He hands Charlie his earbud so that Charlie can keep listening, and suddenly you and Jimmy have semiprivacy. Thank goodness even your teachers are snoozing away, otherwise they'd probably tell you to stay in your seat while the bus is moving. "What's up?"

You look down, studying your shoes in the darkened aisle. "Look, I wanted to apologize for not helping you today, and I know I should have. I just . . . well, I just wanted those passes so badly, I didn't care about anything else for a second." You hold the two passes out to Jimmy, who looks from you to them and back again. "I was going to ask you if you wanted to go with me, but I wouldn't even feel right going now. I thought maybe if you wanted to take"—your voice catches on the next word as if there is a chicken bone caught in your throat—"Mona, you could."

Jimmy takes the passes from you and studies them for a few long moments, letting you sweat it out. But slowly his face goes from neutral to warm. Very warm. He grins up at you and says, "Well, I could . . . but I'd rather take you."

And now you really should go sit down, because your legs suddenly have the consistency of raspberry Jell-O and your heart is thumping loud enough to wake up Mark again.

"Sweet." You smile happily.

"Sweet," Jimmy answers and goes back to listening to his iPod.

You head back to your friends, loving this town even more for the happy ending it just delivered. New York, New York . . . the city so nice they named it twice.

THE END